# MORE PRAISE FOR TOM PICCIRILLI!

"Armed with the cold brilliance of Jim Thompson, the stripped-down language of James M. Cain, and the wry observations of John D. MacDonald, comes Tom Piccirilli, a writer who has staked out the darkest territory of the soul and made it his own."

—*Mystery News*

"Tom Piccirilli never backs away from a disturbing or disgusting scene in the dubious interest of self-censorship, but neither does he seem to relish it as some perverted writers do (guilty, guilty, guilty). He faces it and follows it through to the consequences, and that requires bravery."

—Poppy Z. Brite, author of *Lost Souls*

"What's most fascinating about Piccirilli's work is how successfully he has translated a true sense of the Gothic into very contemporary settings."

—*The Magazine of Fantasy & Science Fiction*

"Finally in Tom Piccirilli we have an American writer who combines a keen knowledge of the writing process with an absolute understanding of how a story needs to be told. His grasp of figurative language and poetic imagery is astounding."

—*Masters of Terror*

# THE CHARNEL HOUSE

Another few minutes and they saw the mansion. Katie tried to find a metaphor that fit, but couldn't quite pull it off. Nothing could do adequate justice to the vista opening before them. This was the charnel house of the Maelstroms. Butchery could be done anywhere, Katie knew, but few places could look like atrocity even from the outside, at night, a decade after.

Drowned moon and lightning gave her only a charcoal sketch of the house, the colonnades silhouetted against the hazy sky. Windows everywhere, some in high standing patterns, others octagonal and stained-glass trapezoids. So weird. Walls ran up into the roof, shingles and clapboards knotted together, architectural styles rapidly changing almost from foot to foot, first floor to second to third. Strange angles played into those gables that could be discerned. Across the third story, settling backwards against the contrasting dormers, there seemed to be columns, porticos of some sort. She imagined that up at the top stood an attic remade into a den: the writing room. . . .

Other *Leisure* books by Tom Piccirilli:
**HEXES**

# THE DECEASED

# TOM PICCIRILLI

LEISURE BOOKS  NEW YORK CITY

*For Michelle, who charms the ghosts from
around my throat.*

A LEISURE BOOK®

August 2000

Published by

Dorchester Publishing Co., Inc.
276 Fifth Avenue
New York, NY 10001

Copyright © 2000 by Tom Piccirilli

ISBN 0-8439-4752-7

Printed in the United States of America.

# THE DECEASED

# *Chapter One*

Laughter and early spring winds breezed past his ear as the words fled across his hands, running like blood.

In the park, Jacob sat under a tree with a stack of spine-snapped paperbacks at his side. He held his father's original manuscript in his lap, yellowed pages full of typos, atrocious misspellings, and all the penciled corrections in his mother's firm and fluent, but often illegible, script. They must have had the same nun for penmanship back in St. Anne of the Blessed Sacrament; who else would be able to understand the scrawls? He read another paragraph and looked up as a cocker spaniel wandered by to sniff cautiously at his shoes.

The setting sun dropped a crimson light forward over the pages of his father's first novel. Jacob reread the words but couldn't get away from the sanguinary imagery, especially here in the final chapter with its innuendo of gore: Dad enjoyed bloodbath finales, his hero walking in to find mason jars with faces in them, internal organs nailed to the ceiling. Strange how his narrative so often leaned toward lyricism, almost as though it had been drawn from a different book too chaste to describe that type of scene. Critics had mentioned that he should have been doing more serious fiction, about relationships and social recourse, as if a kidney on the windowsill weren't serious enough.

The reviewers hadn't said such things about Jacob; some had made the inevitable comparison, and some had gone out of their way not to, but not many were as kind. He put the bulky manuscript back in its folder and picked up one of the paperbacks—also

written by his father—and read the dedication.

> For my wife and children,
> with the only available reason:
> because.

He dropped the book and took another
from the stack. This, his own first novel. He
barely glanced at it, the shadows of the pines
now leaning forward against his neck and
chest, and tossed the paperback aside. He sat
watching the joggers run along the footpaths,
a doubles tennis match finishing up on the
courts with one side clearly upset; a guy snapping at his wife threw his racket into the net.
The cocker spaniel returned, followed by another dog, both leaving in a minute to make
a dash after a Frisbee. A dozen scattered cou-
ples lay entwined on blankets across the
meadow, some with picnics set out, or just a
couple of six-packs. The tennis player picked
up his racket and flung it again. His wife put
her fists on her hips and looked close to moving back in with her mother.

Jacob lay back, enjoying how good the
earth felt against the muscles of his shoulders, stones like eager hands pressing into
him. The wind came on a little stronger with

the approach of night, cooling April's warm weather. Slashes of sunset fell heavily against the branches.

*So, really now, think about it—what else would you expect to see, at this moment, except two kids with identically butchered haircuts standing a couple of feet away from you, each holding a melting ice-cream sandwich, hands, faces, and shirts smeared with vanilla and cookie.* Not twins, he noticed, but similar enough, with almost identical faces.

Jacob's breath hitched, the story already being written in his mind. Sometimes it happened like that, when their lives flapped open to him. *The first simply stared with dark eyes, like any animal that crawled in the mud with its ass in the air, the other with brittle brown shards from a broken beer bottle crushed far into his head, expression submerged in a childish belligerence that would soon become bully-meanness.* You could follow it from there, how it would lead the kid into detention centers, gas-station holdups, and shooting the attendant for no reason, probably using a popcorn .22, walking up to the corpse and still popping it in the face, grinning while he did it. Then to jail and a cell filled with other morons, let out in a couple of years, when he could rape fourteen-year-old Erin at a bus stop, dragging her into the weeds and whittling her face with a box cutter. *Give the brothers names for a minute; how about Clem and Garret.*

"H'lo," said Clem.

Garret stood taller, huskier, more likely the older brother, and for no reason at all turned wildly and smacked the other kid in the side of the head. Jacob grimaced, chewing on his tongue, thinking of his own brother's biceps and the damage they could do despite the gnarled, twiglike legs in the wheelchair.

With brutal zeal Garret drove the remainder of his ice-cream sandwich into his mouth, using his dirty fingers to pull at the sleeve of his ripped sweatshirt and expose a pale, blubbery arm, bending it in a mimed bodybuilder fashion. "Big, huh?"

Jacob nodded, remembering Joseph curling massive barbells the size of Volkswagens, the black veins rising like serpents along his brother's arms.

Dogs barked, and he felt the eyes of the beasts walking in the woods upon him.

Garret cuffed his sibling again with cheerful ease, and actually promenaded his fist under Clem's nose. "Told you I'm stronger than you, didn't I say that? I'm stronger than anyone. You never believe me, but that's what I

11

told you, about me being stronger than anybody else."

"Except Pop."

Flinching, Jacob wondered which of them would recoil first; Clem from the beating that was coming, or maybe the other when Jacob gave it up and let loose the scream that continued to build in his skull.

Joseph, dead ten years with the rest of them, became so close again as this, and Jacob could almost feel the earth moving beneath their backs, all the dust beckoning in the house he'd left.

At last, from down a knoll off by the swings, came the throaty cries of the mother, rushing with an embarrassed smile too wide for those sunken cheeks, too many teeth angled in different directions. *Christ, keep the tale going; you can see she's a Maggie Turner, who prefers Maggie* Tournier, *but she doesn't know how to give it a French-twist accent, originally from Arkansas, and so calls herself Torn-yahy. She sang in the choir as a teenager and cut a demo for fifteen hundred bucks in some recording scam that rooked two or three of her friends. She slept with the producer, a guy named Rawlton, who had grease under his nails because he was really just a mechanic with a garage band on the side.*

Pleasantly plump, Maggie offered a nearly erotic figure. Jacob fingered the paperbacks and wondered if he, or his father, had ever written of her before. She still did a little hooking, at her husband's request, and kept a couple of the dirtier cops in town happy in the backseat of their squad cars, extra cheap half 'n' half action, ten bucks for ten minutes. It wouldn't take longer than that.

She had thick glasses, octagonal lenses, metal frames that looked like you'd need a blowtorch to cut through them. She took them off to repeatedly wipe the bridge of her nose, the harsh focus of the world worn down along the edges, blurred, colors faded, making it easier to breathe day in and day out.

"You two nearly gave me a heart attack, running off without letting me know," she scolded the children, wagging a finger back and forth. "Don't you ever do that to me again, not ever. Promise Mommy you won't do that."

Clem and Garret, perhaps understanding plenty about their own futures and where they'd end up eventually, did not look properly abashed.

With a harrumph, she said to Jacob, "I'm sorry if they disturbed you, mister. They're a little wild sometimes, but they're good kids.

Hope they didn't bother you at all."

He said, "No," and began collecting the books, knowing that escape couldn't be this easy, that everything happened for a purpose, especially now. "No trouble at all."

"Oh, you're a reader, too," the woman cooed, that sort of sound that made your stomach clench, your intestines unwind a little. She tapped her glasses. "Ruined my eyes that way. Seems like nobody reads anymore, except self-help books, which I don't think ever helped anybody much, no matter what they say. What is it you've got here?" She stepped up and pulled out the second-to-last book from the pile under his arm. The publishers had done a good marketing ploy on that one, giving it a Day-Glo orange cover; you could spot it the moment you stepped into the bookstore. He lost his grip on the rest of them and they spilled to the ground, his Dad's manuscript inside the folder splashing with a crumpled-paper sound that painfully struck home.

"Sorry," she said, staring at the fanged creature on the cover, its arm outstretched toward the reader, the way his sister Rachel used to do, and with a similar smile. It was a stupid picture, but had helped to sell the book—he never understood why. "Oh God,

Isaac Maelstrom. He's my absolute . . ." *Uh-huh*. Jacob knew; he could hear the way she'd stretch the word out like exceptionally sweet taffy. *Jesus, no*. ". . . *fay-vor-eet!* His books are so scary. Even his name is creepy, you got to love that. It can't be real, don't you think? They like doing that, changing their names all the time, like actors. He must've."

Jacob whispered, "Yes." It had been rewritten, edited down from Malstromo, by his great-great-grandfather Thaddeus, called Taddy and sometimes Teddy, who'd captained a whaling vessel and slave ships, averaging sixty barrels of oil per voyage out around Cape Horn and Drake's Passage, taking no more than two hundred slaves on his ship and losing hardly a sixth of them to disease in the holds.

The woman's heavy blouse and pancake makeup did not entirely cover the number of bruises covering her shoulders and neck, discolorations ranging from cinnamon to blue-black. The guy had big fist, but not as big as Joseph's. It looked like he was a lefty, knuckle marks appearing most often on the right side of her.

"And the way him and his family died, wasn't it awful? I mean, you read about it and you think in a way it's ironic, but then it makes sense, too, this guy with that kind of stuff crawling around in his head." She touched his hand as though sharing a solemn moment with him.

It was darker now, sun having almost melted into the horizon. The lamps in the park came to dim life, lights on the ball field already turned up as the players tossed the ball around. The moon climbed, a lean three-quarters full.

"Momma, I'm stronger than anybody," Garret said, the box cutter and screaming little girl so clear in Jacob's mind that his throat went dry. "Right?"

"Right, dear, of course you are."

"I knew it."

"It's time to go," Clem noted with an emotionless, fishlike expression. "Before Pop kicks the shit out of us."

She waved them off, rifling through the other books in his hands. It felt as if she clawed deeper than that, eviscerating him, licking her thumb to turn the pages, to pluck at his guts. "And Jacob Maelstrom!" She hugged the novel to her chest, and for a breathless instant he felt as if it were actually him being snuggled tightly in that gaping, bruised cleavage. His hands weren't half as large as her husband's or his brother's; he wouldn't know how to please her. "Oh, he's pretty good, too, not like his father, but it must run in the family that way. All that history."

*This is called exposition,* he recalled his father explaining to him, Rachel leaning over his shoulder, breathing in his ear, reading the papers spread out on the table as his father grinned. *It's an immature yet useful tool when the writer needs to define the conflict early on and drive it directly into the foreground of the narrative. It's a cheap shortcut; don't bother with it.* He saw Rachel's hand on his pages, her nails leaving impressions behind, as they left their marks on him, too.

The woman grabbed the copy of his latest novel from him, *Sins of the Sons,* and turned it over in her hands, muttering about the ferocious ending. He wanted to urge her to go home. Garrett was right; her husband was just going to beat the shit out of her again. She checked the inside back cover and spotted the black and white photo, still relatively new to most mass-market paperbacks. She looked at him with a hard squinting and back again to the photo, then did it again until realization registered in her face.

The deciding factors were the darkness and her poor vision. She never would have recognized him from the grainy shot if she'd found him twenty minutes earlier in the sunlight. The photograph had been taken in a neighborhood bar, and shadows loomed in it much more than his face did, slightly out-of-focus because he'd been turning toward someone shouting his name. His publisher sometimes set him up like that, came after him when he didn't fill out the publicity sheets and mail them back. The park lamp nearest them gave off about the same shine as the low lights in the bar.

"It's you," she whispered, letting the novel hang from her fingers, the crease in the spine growing as he darted his hand out and snatched the book from her. He put it back under his arm with the rest. He'd seen adolescents get this way around the vampire writers, fans dressed in black robes and whiteface, a specially designed set of dentures inserted, made from human teeth, with tattoos of comic book characters and the grim reaper blazing on their necks and shoulders; everyone was hypnotized because they needed to discover myth so desperately.

"It's me," he said. "Nice meeting you. Goodbye." He walked sideways across the unearthed roots of the maples, heading backward for the garden path. Far ahead, the cocker spaniel continued to romp.

"Wait! Wait! Mr. Maelstrom!"

*Good Christ, Mr. Maelstrom.* He grimaced at the alliteration of his own name. It sounded so melodramatic—she was right— like a stage persona. How could it be that none of them had switched it to Smith or Jones or Strumm; why did Thaddeus still hold sway?

She came over and gripped his shoulder with a brutal pinch, got a nice handful of his flesh, and whirled him around to face her. Damn, she was strong, this lady; she had to be to put up with her husband. "I thought *Surgery of the Claw* was positively devastating, I stayed up till all hours of the night for a week afterward, I'm telling you. The way you did those scenes, with the guy tied to the bed, all those knives hanging above him, and then the two killers going after one another with the . . . what were they . . . those stiletto things. And that other chapter, where the crazy kid goes home and sticks his head in the oven and his face sorta just melts off. God, that gave me nightmares; it really did. . . . You're fantastic."

He wondered if her kids might not even make it to juvenile court. Jacob smiled impeccably. "Thank you."

Tom Piccirilli

"You're welcome; you're very welcome."

He felt the reality of all his father's words, their weight and substance alive and menacing, fighting with his own sentences, here in his hand. He rubbed at the back of his neck, the headache coming on swiftly.

"I think you're almost as good as your father," she said.

With his grin pulling a little tighter now, but still no inflection at all, he repeated himself. "Thank you."

She crossed her arms under her breasts, lifting them out of habit, a strange gesture of invitation. He could imagine her bra slung over his couch, the bite marks and welts on her belly and back so terrible in their detail. His stomach twisted. She said, "Would you mind if I asked you a question?"

He chewed his fillings together. "Look, it's been very pleasant talking to you, but I have to be going."

"It's important to me. Maybe you wouldn't really understand, but listen, I'd really just like to say—"

"Sorry, it's late. I've got a lot of work to do."

"Please, won't take a second."

"I—"

"Please."

*Of course, and here it comes. Like always,*

20

*just like forever.* Endless questions because he had nothing better to do, everybody giving him the same buddy-buddy, shoulder-to-shoulder curiosity act like they were all best friends about to go out to a hockey game. It was the way the reporters had played him, the cops, and the psychiatrists, too. Each of them giving him the eyes that said, *You can tell* me. He'd seen it a hundred times before, beginning when he was eleven. But he couldn't tell them anything, because he didn't know. Hell, he was still waiting for someone to tell *him.* They all wanted minutiae, urged him to be as graphic as possible: the doctors came out with Magic Markers and reams of paper, maybe one blue marker, one green, and five red ones, like they expected him to use it most, drawing the carnage. After the doctors it was the editors, interviewers, and the types of ladies who would yank on his shoulder. Everyone pretending confidence, leaning in with a grin to ask: What happened to them? Why did your sister do it? What did you see? Why are you alive? What did she do with their heads?

"Where do you get your ideas from?"

He gave a soft grunt and nearly vomited. It wasn't a relief to hear that instead—he got his ideas the same way everyone did, by being who he was, by asking his own questions. He fumbled for an answer, not wanting to say anything. Looking into her eyes he wondered just when the hell her husband would butcher her, when the kids would turn on her, when some backseat john who didn't like it enough would smash her face against the dashboard.

The corpse-eyed boy said, "Pop's gonna beat the shit outta us, Momma. We gotta go. Come on!"

"In a minute, dear."

"He's gonna kill us."

Jacob believed the kid. He backpedaled a few steps, spun, and quickly walked away, empty of almost everything except the directionless need for flight. The voices were back again all of a sudden, springing on him after all these years. Paragraphs of Dad's novels poured out of him by rote. The books quivered, alive as they could be, his own words loving—or perhaps at war with—his father's, being murdered by them just as he should have been killed ten years ago.

The anniversary was coming up, and Jacob knew he had to go back and find out the truth behind this dead enemy that had once been called his family.

# *Chapter Two*

They called him. They were always calling him.

The force of their presence weighed heaviest just before he fell asleep, and again in the morning as he drifted awake. In the back of his neck that familiar sensation began, tightness in his forehead alerting him to the undertow of nightmare about to drag him down, but by now it was too late to do anything about it.

## Tom Piccirilli

They crept from their deaths into his porous dreams. Words, faces, voices. The noises he hadn't heard for such a long time in the world: morning greetings, breakfast-table clatter, forks striking dishes, and the slurp of coffee. The squeak of the wheelchair rolling along the carpet, and the faint humming from his sister as she followed the tunes of birds in the boughs outside the dining-room window.

Jacob saw his own body flicker into focus within the nightmare, light warping and writhing around his frame as he came into being among them. Molecules bounced, pieces of himself carefully, almost cautiously, unwinding into existence as his family turned in their chairs to look at him.

He was partly presently here and partly uneasily there, until he sat having breakfast staring at them, back home on Stonethrow Island. He looked at his reflection in the silverware and grunted. "Uh-oh."

More symbolic and sensual, this haunting, than others he'd researched, where furniture spun against the ceiling. He didn't know what the hell to do, so he just smiled pleasantly, waiting for them to start.

His father grinned there before him now, but at the same time Dad was upstairs in his attic study, steadily clacking away at his ancient portable Underwood that left dropped *Q*s and flying *T*s angled oddly over every page. The constant metallic, biting sounds of the typing seemed to soothe Mom as she stared hopefully up the stairs, calling for his father to come down to eat. Dad, already here, looked across the plates at him with no discernible expression, nothing angry or sad, only searching, almost rosy with sympathy. The face of Isaac Maelstrom had grown ruddier than Jacob remembered, black hair salted at the temples with thin gray streaks the man hadn't lived long enough to acquire.

The grandfather clock in the parlor tolled eight, and the squirrels and birds made a ruckus at the windowsill. Jacob shuddered in his seat—also sweating in his bed—watching as Rachel eased into the seat beside him, turned her gorgeous eyes on him, and asked when he'd be coming home.

Six years older than he, she remained stuck at a dead seventeen. She hadn't opted to age as their father had; her smooth, welcoming smile remained line by line the same as ever— crisp humor, kindness, and something inextricably bitter married there, the white gleam of her teeth appealing but also appalling in a way. Her long black hair curled in a way she

25

had sometimes worn it on holidays or when her usual ponytail didn't meet up to the occasion. Annoyed by his lack of response, she repeated with half a smirk, *When?*

"But I'm right here," Jacob said.

She shifted closer, lifted her fork, and scooped some of the eggs from her dish into his mouth. He gagged on the complexity of taste, the awful smell of it in the middle of the nightmare, in the darkness, such solidity unexpected. She laughed as he choked, then wiped his chin for him and said, *I know that, silly! But you've just got to come visit us more often; you're always so God damn busy—*

*Rachel,* Mom flatly warned, her eyes terrified, as though every bit of her will was battling for release, tears shining there. *Curb the trash mouth, please.*

Jesus, their mother, somehow . . . even she couldn't get free.

*Sorry, Mother. She turned back to Jacob. You're always so darned busy that it's about time someone told you what you already know. Get it into that thick, wonderful, genius brain of yours that we love you and want you to visit more often. We've all missed you, isn't that right, Mom?*

*Very much,* Mom answered, a hiss escaping, as though each ersatz breath had to be driven into and out of her. *You should come around more often.*

Jacob sought out sincerity and couldn't find any; his mother had been squeezed slimmer now, older, yet more attractive in a proud fashion. Her smile looked forced, as though somebody held a gun to the back of her head but told her to remain calm, as though this were killing her all over again. The hinges of her jaws were pinched white, her ridiculously cheesy smile never reaching her agonized gaze.

*Your room hasn't even been touched, Third,* Rachel pressured, calling him by the dreaded nickname. She'd throw it out again in a second. *It's exactly as you left it, Third, and you can work on your novels-in-progress when you need to, and tour the orchards and caves when you have time. Please think about coming this weekend, will you, promise?* She giggled her particular laugh that eased up under his ribs like fingers tickling him. Another forkful of eggs came edging toward his mouth.

Jacob blocked it with his hand, relishing the physical contact, his nerves burning. Rachel's smile widened, and she cocked her head, giving him that sloe-eyed gaze. Her teeth had been ready to bite as she leaned in closer, set on chewing or kissing him. He said, "That's enough. . . ."

In a moment, he smelled his brother's aftershave.

Remotely aware of the numbness now lapping at his legs, Jacob pressed forward to accept Rachel's lips. He needed to see just how much of her was really left, and how much she could still affect him. He opened his mouth and abruptly found himself in Joseph's wheelchair, rolling backward into the parlor.

Joseph stood by the fireplace, beneath the portraits of their parents and grandparents and other ancestors. Up there, Taddy glared at the world, looking furious about the dead slaves he couldn't sell, and the whales he never brought in. Joseph's massive arms came close to shredding the short-sleeved shirt he wore, his skeletal legs now changed into healthy limbs, corded and substantial. He, too, had declined getting older; perhaps he'd even allowed himself to become a little younger. Jacob thought they were about the same age now.

"Any particular reason why you're playing these games?" Jacob asked. "Would it have made you feel better if I'd been crippled, too?" He knew it wouldn't have, but couldn't move from the chair. Lame now, he felt his brother's familiar rage, revenge-bent but without meaning. Jacob hadn't even been born when Joseph had decided to dive head-long from one branch of a pine to another, whooping like Tarzan, not even close to completing the leap, only about ten or twelve feet short. What did he think . . . that the tree was going to reach out and grab him?

*Of course*, Joseph said. *There are always reasons, Third.* Standing in front of Jacob, arms crossed over his iron chest, he looked as though he could burst the world into fragments. He grinned, boyish and amiable, and for an instant Jacob imagined them as friends, the sentiment rising but memories impeding it. Joseph knew it, too; his head filled with the same thoughts, imagining the soil roiling beneath the three of them, and his grin shifted to a leer of disdain. He sat at the piano and played, with a couple of seconds' pause between notes, as though he were hesitant in the playing of his song or unsure of where each key lay, distracted or afraid of touching the ivory.

Once or twice, Jacob had seen brothers who were really friends, having beers and actually laughing together. But maybe he'd only imagined it, although he was certain he'd never written such a scene. He willed his legs back, watching as the details of his body rearranged once more, like words flowing one after the other, being rewritten along the way. The clacking of a typewriter filled the room. He stood from the wheelchair, braced his foot against the seat, and kicked viciously, sending it down the hallway, where it vanished among the shadows and gloom of the house. He walked back into the dining room, where the four corpses waited for him.

"What do you want from me?" he asked.

*Nothing.* Joseph sighed as the earth thickened across his face, his eyes going first, inch by inch, worms burrowing, entering and exiting.

"Oh, that's cute."

*Nothing, darling,* Mom said, her voice packed with sorrow. The muscles in her face jerked, as if wires were being tugged somewhere offstage. *We only want to be together again, the same as you want.* Her mouth kept moving, but her words were deleted. What was she telling him? Her skin shrank away to reveal patches of bone, and her tongue dissolved into black liquid that dripped onto the linen tablecloth.

Composition and decomposition; Rachel's beautiful features began to crumble, but she remained too vain to spoil her face for such a bargain effect. "Now, that's better," Jacob said. He couldn't help but snicker—despite murder, some things never changed. She grimaced, then snarled, stuck out her bottom lip, and pouted, caught halfway between disgust and seduction.

Dad sat.

His father had answers but couldn't provide them. The man would not lie, though he had built his career on lies, twisting the carefully conceived truths of life, carving off pieces of them all, and twisting and subverting all memory and history, even myth. Dad approached him, but faded from sight just as they were about to meet. An oddly echoing question trailed behind: *Why are you doing this to yourself?*

Jacob rushed to Rachel, her face partially marred but so gorgeous, too, her soul finally coming to the surface. "Enough of this crap. You've got something to say, well, so do I. Tell me, Rachel. I want to know why you did it."

*I didn't do anything.*

"And tell me why you didn't finish me the same way."

*You already know.*

"I can't remember."

*Well, my, isn't that convenient?* The blood

31

burned through her face. *Why not ask your little girlfriend? Better yet, come home and find out.*

He lifted her partially decayed chin until their noses touched.

"You've got it," Jacob said.

# Chapter Three

Wakely had a way of dropping into slow motion just before he blew his stack and started flinging nonbreakable stuff around his office.

Most people who knew him correctly assumed that he'd learned the theatrical posturing from watching so many of the grade-B action flicks made from the novels he'd agented. It seemed like every third or fourth book had the same plot, where a nice guy gets pushed too far and the cameras go in for a close-up on the seething eyes, the groaning music rushing upward into a squeal of violin strings and blaring trumpets, the gratuitous explosion of oiled pectorals and violence. He got passes to the openings and used to go all the time before the flicks downshifted into straight-to-video releases and became too low-budget even to have openings.

He flung papers mostly. He wasn't even tearing them or crumpling them into balls in his fists—just yanking the fill from the printer tray and sailing them around. "No," Wakely said. "No, you are not." He didn't have much muscle, and the highest order of violence he'd ever done outside of shot-putting trash around his office was to place a loaded bottle of Jack Daniel's to his head. Wagging his chin, he plucked at the white river that threaded through his beard, smoothed back a few of the oncoming wrinkles at his neck. "You cannot be serious."

"Of course I am, Bob."

"Yeah, I know; that was a stupid thing to say."

Wakely started getting into it, just as he always did, beginning with a cool resignation that he soon lost, huffing and screwing up his lips, going for the wastepaper basket first, giving it a misjudged kick with the point of his shoe but not even knocking it over. Papers on his desk were next, but they were too important; he made a production of acting as if he were carelessly tossing them, but he really only moved top sheets from here to there and back again. The paper tray he just sort of grabbed and plopped down once more. The room, which was too cold, filled with a syrupy pause.

Back to the garbage, this time booting it with the side of his foot, spilling some onto the carpet, still huffing, doing a little flamenco on the crap for a minute. It was hard to respect but easy to love a man like this, the total antithesis of Isaac Maelstrom. "Uh, yeah, you really are. You're out of your mind if you think I'm going to let you do it, like it shouldn't matter."

"Look, Bob—"

"Hey, I don't give lectures, you know I don't give lectures, but this is something else totally."

"Yes, it is."

"I thought we had an understanding that you'd never go back there."

"We did."

"Was I wrong about that?"

"No, you were right."

"Tell me if I was wrong."

"You were right."

"Jesus Christ, stop agreeing with me."

Jacob got an embarrassed and politely con-doling look from Wakely's newest secretary, Lisa. He liked her already because she chose to sit next to Jacob on the couch when it would have been easier for her to take the chair across from Bob. A redheaded lady who stood six feet in flats, only a year or two out of college, she didn't insist on being called a receptionist or an assistant or an office man-ager. She had a nice fullness in the cheeks, caramel freckles she didn't lighten with makeup, and her ears weren't pierced, which he found slightly exotic. She tried for a straight face but kept giving him sidelong glances, as if she knew this act already and still got a kick out of it. Her mouth shifted into a smirk, the kind only a lover would dare to give, and Jacob knew Wakely was sleeping with her.

Lisa moved her steno pad into her lap—pages covered with vicious swirls like no shorthand he knew—and crossed her mer-cury legs, which looked like they could kick the shit out of any would-be attacker. He wondered how many times Wakely's back had been thrown out in recent weeks. She cocked her head, watching Wakely doing a sort of funky chicken now, a little salsa beat in there.

"I didn't think anybody used them anymore," Jacob said.

"What?" Lisa asked.

"Steno pads and shorthand."

"I'm not too good with computers yet."

"Neither am I."

"To tell you the truth, I hate them."

"Me, too."

"You must be Jacob," she said.

He nodded. Their bare arms touched as they sat together on the couch, and he started getting entranced by her hair, the way it feathered against him. "I guess Bob's told you a little about me?"

"A little. Does he always do this when you show up to say hello?"

"Venting is good for the soul," he said.

"I'm Lisa Hawkings. I'm a big fan. I've read all of your books."

He'd never seen a worse poker face in his life—her eyes actually bugged, the corners of her mouth dipping into a guilty simper. He held his hand out, still pretty uncertain whether it was socially acceptable to really shake hands with a woman. She took it, though, scratching lightly up his wrist. Her fist was bigger than his. "Thank you, Lisa."

"You know I'm lying."

"Yes, I know."

"How do you do that?"

Wakely straightened his papers, sat, and glanced over, appearing pensive and frightened. He slowly spun in the chair, his knees jittery. Jacob knew all his moves, but this was a new one. Even Lisa shrugged, unsure exactly what the guys were talking about, though she must have known some of it.

Robert Wakely, his father's agent and now his own, had been a sort of uncle who came around a lot when Jacob was a kid. He had fought to become his legal guardian during a custody battle brought on by a great-aunt from out of the farthest branches of the Malstromo family tree. He'd met her once, a sweet and genuine woman, but she was over sixty and didn't need an eleven-year-old in her life. She gave him a handful of homemade fudge and a couple of photos of his father as a kid playing with a bunch of other kids. They all looked angry. Jacob and Wakely lived together as amicable but distant roommates for the next seven years, until Jacob turned eighteen and came into his inheritance.

Robert Wakely had written three books about his father, the first two hitting the best-seller list because everyone hoped he'd have some inside knowledge about the murders. He'd managed to get his hands on a few of the actual crime scene photos, but the bodies themselves had been whited out in the frame so that there was nothing to see. Still, you couldn't help but notice that all the silhouettes ended at the neck. By the third book, though, people realized he'd only reiterate his personal accounts and a give a little analysis on Isaac Maelstrom's career and the generally bad movies made from the prose, and that Wakely really couldn't write worth a damn because he wouldn't allow Jacob to edit for him.

Lisa said, "Why don't I get some lunch for everyone?"

"That would be nice," Jacob said. "Thank you." He'd be long gone before she returned, and she understood the fact.

"Thanks," Wakely said. "I think that's just what we need. Have a meal, a few cocktails. How about if we go out to Spivey's; is that all right with everyone?"

He'd missed the point, or had rationalized it away. Lisa knew it, too, and acted as if she hadn't heard him. She left without saying another word, playing the part out, and Jacob liked her even better.

Wakely plucked at his beard some more. "Don't go back."

"Why?"

"Listen, I'm not getting into it again."

"Yes, you are," Jacob said. "You have been since the minute I walked in, but that's okay; I understand."

"Don't patronize me."

"I'm not."

"Your father used to do that shit."

"But I don't."

"Like hell."

"If we get into this we might not ever get out of it, Bob."

Wakely knew it was true. "Look, it's ridiculous to even discuss it. We put that madness behind us years ago. Now you seem determined to haunt yourself, and there's no justification for it. You still haven't given me an adequate reason for why you want to put yourself through this. Inspiration? You don't need any more inspiration; you've got more behind you than anybody." Wakely's voice ran out from under him, so that he had to take a deep breath. "Are you finally going to accept one of the true-crime lines on their offer to write a nonfiction book? After all this time?"

"Tell me how long you've been in love with Lisa."

"Uh, yeah, uh, yeah, that's wonderful." Wakely spun in his seat again, his knees still bouncing. It kind of looked like fun. "That's just wonderful. At least two weeks. Now quit avoiding my question."

"I like her, and I'm not avoiding the question. It was stupid of you to ask. You already know I'd never write about that house."

"Yes, you would—it's what you do; you've just been waiting for the right time to do it. And now it'll be a decade, and that seems significant, doesn't it?" Not really, no more than nine years or eight or eleven, but Wakely had obviously been thinking a lot about it. Maybe he wanted to try another book; there had been a posthumous Isaac Maelstrom novel and a miniseries since the last one. "A ten-year retrospective, looking back on bloodshed—well, forget that. I forbid it."

"You do."

"Yes."

"You forbid it."

"Fucking A right, you listening to me? You mocking me? I forbid it." He actually sounded as if he was trying to sound tough, solicitous, and paternal for a moment, but then, with an ineffable sadness that shook his

41

voice and caught them both off guard, Wakely added, "I've . . . I've tried to be a good father to you."

"Oh, Christ, Bob," Jacob blurted. "Not that; please don't start getting into that." He winced at the unexpected bluntness of affection, and found it almost horrifying in its implications, so far off the track of their relationship.

"Listen, everybody is going to be camping out and watching you on this one. You know the anniversary has brought a resurgence of interest in the field and your name. Everyone and his brother wants to cash in on your success. And you've leased Stonethrow to so many other authors in the past that they'll be giving interviews all over the place, and writing their own memoirs about Isaac and their time spent in that goddamn house."

Yes, that was the idea exactly. Get them out there tapping into the place, hoping they would steal away with some of the arcana coiled inside the home, siphon off their power. "Those writers were Dad's friends, and some of them are yours and mine, as well, Bob. They won't be back, and they respect us and themselves enough not to turn the resurgence of the genre into a circus."

"That's exceedingly naive of you, Jacob."

"If fans show up I don't care about signing a few books . . . but no one will show. Nobody even knows where Stonethrow is."

"And it's foolhardy, too. You don't know who'll be there. Lisa fields calls every couple of hours, and she doesn't even know the whole story about . . ."

*Ellipses*, Dad had said, *are used to leave the reader afloat in a pause of connotation, with the understanding that revelation is about to unfold, creeping forward but not quite there yet. But about to spring soon.*

Wakely came over and sat beside him. They were too close now in their shared anxiety, much closer than they'd ever been in the years Jacob had lived in Wakely's home, listening to the one-night stands, all the goddamn disco albums. "I never asked what happened. . . ."

"Bob."

"I don't want you to think it was because I didn't care. . . ."

"That's enough."

"I do, I do love you, though I know I never showed it much, I realize that, but I'm willing to listen if you ever want to talk."

"No."

"I think you can handle whatever's left for you at Stonethrow, but I can't. Maybe I'm superstitious. . . ." He wasn't. Jacob had once seen him hit on a novice nun, one of the new sisters who got to wear the cute little dresses and keep her hair down. "Not like I believe everything that Dionne Warwick tells me over the Psychic Friends phone network, or the stuff that you put into your stories, but, listen . . . I had a dream last night."

*God, no.*

Impossible. They couldn't have come all this way out of the mud. Jacob wondered if he might make it to the door in time, if there was still a chance of escape.

"Bob . . ."

Wakely could do the unexpected and perform magic; he'd freak over nothing and handle a high-six-figure deal with a cool disposition, skillfully choosing the precise words to make everything work perfectly. His calm demeanor now made Jacob break into a frosty sweat. Wakely said, "I woke up screaming—that sounds like an exaggeration, right? No matter how bad a nightmare you never really wake up screaming. But the sheets were soaking, and I was sitting up, and I shrieked until my throat gave out, I'm telling you. Dionne never said anything about that. Your father—"

"Shut the fuck up."

"She's pregnant, you know," Wakely said. "Lisa's pregnant; I'm going to marry her. Your father asked me to tell you that you shouldn't keep doing this to yourself. He ordered me to stay away. Rachel was there, too, the exact way I remember. Jesus Christ, you don't know. It was awful; you don't know." Of course Jacob knew. "Christ, I'm scared."

So it hadn't been his choice to go back home. *Everything happens for a reason.* The threads of the net had been knotting and tightening all the time.

"Who else was there?" Jacob asked.

"A little girl, some little girl, and she says she's dying."

# *Chapter Four*

Lisa crossed the street, moving against the suddenly rude crush of a crowd heading in the opposite direction. A couple of Chinese delivery boys with death in their eyes sped by as though they wanted to ride over somebody's throat. She stepped up on the curb and wove her way into the corner cafeteria, already smelling the coffee above the stench of the piled garbage outside.

A group of badly dressed businessmen elbowed each other at her entrance, some of them smiling pleasantly, others with love handles unrolling over their wrinkled slacks, only chortling, a gruff sound she usually hated, but for some reason didn't mind so much at the moment. She checked the menu and ordered a low-fat meal for Bob, hoping to get his cholesterol down a little. She knew Jacob would be long gone by the time she returned.

While the counterman worked she moved to the pay phone near the rest rooms, briskly walking past the same businessmen again, giving it a near strut with some Mae West tushie wag thrown in for fun, and grinned deliberately enough that they all grew intimidated and hid their faces in their BLTs.

She picked up the receiver, clamped a hand over her free ear to fend off the din of the cafeteria, dialed, and got Katie's answering machine. She shook her head, amazed that Katie still went to her nine A.M. history class on the Philippines in the 1920s. Not so long ago, Lisa had felt ashamed that she'd never had the finances or the grades to go to college. It used to eat at her when people asked what she'd majored in, what her alma mater was, and they'd show off their Phi Beta Kappa keys and graduation rings and talk about sororities. But after hearing that they actually gave classes where you studied things like the Philippines in the 1920s, she felt a swell of relief that she hadn't wasted her time or money.

Maybe Katie hadn't attended the lecture, and had instead opted to hit her new napping place, the university library, where she had taken to crapping out on the new futons lining the windows on the third floor. That proved to be near the Philippines texts but far enough out of the way that there weren't too many interruptions from either the staff or the students. Lisa had met her for drinks after work and knew where to find her. Katie usually kept her feet propped on her brightly colored notebooks, everything with properly coded tabs and folders, organized into anal-retentive achievement, all for a Humanities degree that would set her hopelessly adrift in the hunt for a job. Katie's thesis, though, would be locked under her arm even while she napped, as if an ax murderer would have to shear her at the shoulder to get to it. Lisa sometimes got a rush of superiority when she thought about how many of the collegians would be chasing after anything as prestigious as her own job when they got out from behind their Ivy-covered walls.

". . . and I'll get back to you as soon as I can. Thanks!"

Lisa said, "Katie, how foolish you are going to feel, having gone to crawl around those dusty shelves stuffed with Filipinos, when you listen to this. The Fates have conspired in your favor again. I'm not changing the topic, but I wanted to tell you that you were right: I think I'm falling in love, damn it, and don't remind me that I get attached too quickly to the wrong kind of man, all right? I mean, don't I know that already? And yeah, he's too old for me, but we'll talk about all this when we've got a couple of Long Island iced teas in front of us."

She still didn't know how much to tell Katie, what the completely safe topics were, what she should go into detail about and what she should hold back on. At times they could talk about men and children and houses, porches and money and birth control and their brothers and mothers. And sometimes they approached a subject and Lisa could see her friend's face shifting as if she'd been smacked, her eyes starting to glaze over because it took her back to her bad days with Grandpa, or Tim and the shit that finally sidewinded her into the hospital.

"Anyway, so after I luckily fall into the employment of one Robert Wakely Literary Agency, Inc., forgetting about the terrific sex for the moment, and hand you over signed copies of his books about the Maelstrom Massacre, guess who walks in today but a certain hermit writer you've been dying to interview for however long it's been, only to meet with rejection and rebuff ad nauseam, despite my pleas and using some of my wilier charms upon my Bobby. He's got willpower. Hey, no shit, it just so happens I know where your dissertation subject is going to be this weekend, and we can turn it into a girls' night out kind of thing, I think." She wondered if any of this would be enough to save Katie. "It's only a couple hours upstate. He seems really nice and easygoing, too, not uptight like Bob at all. And Katie, forget that crappy photo they use on the back cover of his books; he's actually kinda cute."

She hung up the phone, went to the ladies' room, locked herself in a stall, and went into a silent crying jag for about ninety seconds. When she was through she just needed a little eyeliner for touch up. She wondered if Bob would pay for at least half the abortion.

# *Chapter Five*

With the same affirmation that lost lovers feel
for one another's flesh, his feet fell in contact
with the subtle shifting of the dirt.

Leaves lapped at his ankles, earth perhaps
moving up to meet his step. Stonethrow soil
seemed to welcome him back, and an odd
sense of pride welled within him.

Pond water rippled, the moon's reflection
tilted and bobbing; these restless motions
meant something large still swam in there.

Jacob knelt at the shore and swept his fingers through the scum surface, waiting for a touch reaching up from below, one that didn't come. A distant splashing in the dark water beat out a rhythmic tune of flailing, like the arms and legs of a drowning woman tumbling deeper and deeper into the weeds. He turned his back to it and walked to his car.

The wet road drank the Corvette's headlights as he slowly drove to the house. He clicked off the defogger and rolled down the window, listening to the rapids groaning and roaring behind him, thrumming heavily through the forest.

Stonethrow Island's name was apt, as were all the words his father put to things. Four square miles of a diamond-shaped tract of land snuggled among mountains and cliffs, surrounded by a pair of rivers, each split into two channels by the northeast and southwest points of the island. Rapids coursed violently around its borders, effectively cutting Stonethrow off from the mainland, thrashing runnels all around, where the four rivulets again converged and fell back into two raging veins at their opposing ends. Crashing headlong into each other, they became separate waterfalls that spilled back down to sea level as the cascade emptied into a swollen lake a couple of miles off.

The mainland extended into the world a scant hundred yards across the bridge he'd just driven, set over the eastern branch of the river. Beyond it the mountains rose into timber country and poky trails, other dirt roads that occasionally grew over and were cut back by the few men who still used them.

If you were trained and talented enough, and had any inclination to do so, you could get across the bridge, wander the western branch, and, using nylon ropes and carabiners, climb down the slope of cliffs and tramp to a series of mill towns, the most prominent of which remained Gallows, made famous as the setting for most of his father's interlocking novels. He had packed demons behind the windows—twin sons of alien parents, modern-day witches and their acerbic familiars, pigs that ran rampant, and killers who cruised the highways searching for their stolen souls. One of his hardbacks contained a map showing how his hero had climbed down the cliff into the circle of hell. A couple of teenagers had tried to do so about five years ago, got hung up on the rocks, and had to be rescued by rangers.

Headlights washed against the carport and

garage. Its smudged, cracked windows gave back little glare. As he suspected, there were no fans awaiting him. No interviewers or cameramen, or networks doing follow-up stories, showing the edited, silhouette crime-scene photos again. Stonethrow remained, as did all Maelstrom possessions—loyalty, affection, pain, and desire—removed from the rest of the world. That was what had made the games so easy to play.

Jacob parked, grabbed his camping lantern from out of the trunk, checked the garage and found the drum of fuel in the corner. He knocked on the metal tank and heard that it was full. It must have been out here seven or eight months at least. The last author who'd rented the place had moved out in early autumn but had never sold his latest horror novel. Even Wakely thought it was too much of a downer.

Jacob poured gas into the generator, checked the oil and decided it was clean enough, pressed the primer, and worked the cord until the motor purred. A light overhead sparked to golden life.

Intensely grateful, but equally surprised, he wondered why he stood so calmly rooted now, even as he gazed at the empty space on the wall. . . . His father had always been so careful about replacing tools in their proper places. It held his attention as profoundly as anything else his sister had ever put on view, this marked outline in the clapboard where three carefully placed hooks waited to again hold an ax.

He flicked the relay switch that would power the house, exited, and walked to the porch, not wanting to think.

An odd smell instantly recognizable wafted into his face: lilies. Wind brought the scent a long way from his mother's field, where the flowers had grown wildly, her paring and re-planting doing nothing to keep the garden at bay. He took jagged breaths, testing the air, the fragrance pure and unmistakable. He nearly afforded himself a grin, recalling his mom in her overalls about ten sizes too big, dabs of dirt on her hands and chin and the tip of her nose, weeds in her hair.

Like a warbling shout in his ear, the memories came swarming loudly from every angle. He spun toward voices, laughter, and Rachel's shrieks. At once, the night surrounding him abruptly peeled back, sunlight and other seasons pouring through in patches. He saw different portions of various events occurring around him, as if the world were actually old wallpaper fastened against the universe, with ripped scraps showing through in spots. Beneath the night he could see different years running on and on, hidden like old pictures painted over by the present. He reached out as if to grab the rotting layer of today and tack it back into place, burying the dead past again down where it belonged.

Lightning split his skull.

Jacob screamed and fell to his knees, something inside getting out again, and what had been driven outside getting back in. The high-powered lantern rolled from his grasp. In the woods, to his left, he heard weeping. They were always crying.

"Not again . . ." he said in a growl, blood filling his mouth.

From a rustling in the brush he heard a girl's squeal and rushing footsteps; he thought—almost hoped—that maybe he'd been shot, an insane fan with a .22 blaming her lonely nightmares on him. More blood poured from his nose, spattering the ground. He checked his head and chest, finding no wounds. He stood and stumbled for the tree line, his hackles rising as the tittering kept on going, taking more breath than anyone should be able to do. Wheeling, he searched the brush and foolishly called out, "Who's there?" in a heated, desperate whisper. As if they might actually answer, as if they could tell him what he needed to know. Movement in his peripheral vision drew his attention, and Jacob spun, seeing nothing in the darkness except his childhood. The lilies tugged heavily at his lungs until he gasped, and he slowly slid to the ground again.

It had happened like this before, with blood streaming down his face. Torn edges of darkness revealed the days he didn't want to remember. His stomach felt like nothing more than an empty sack filling with despair, his forehead itchy and dirty as it met with other wills, unanswered prayers, and unrequited love. It had happened like this before, out in the black woods. Sorrow trying to get at him, as well as anguish and longing. . . .

But not his family's, and not only his, either. Not exactly . . .

It had happened like this before: a different form of demand that had been waiting for release. The laughter drifted, directionless but near, and was now joined by even more voices. Men and women, perhaps many or only a few, he couldn't tell from the muttered grumbles that rose around him or the strange, chanting cries, like children humming over a dead pet. This had somehow become a solemn moment. All that lingered out there had spent years in the night scratching and sniffing, and now waited to exact a toll, proclaiming that nothing mattered now beyond the *need* to live out a promise of life that had been made. It raged in the woods and clattered in the branches above him, drawing him farther into the depths of the maelstrom. Unknown neurochemicals slithered in his cerebral cortex.

Furious shadows gliding in moonlight made him realize that something had been missing from inside the man he had become, continuing to live beyond him but still taking passionate bites. Stonethrow, alive and hungry. Lovers moved in on him: in love, needing love, and eager to give him love. The skunk with its ass in the air, his brother crawling in the mud.

He began to sob uncontrollably, trying to get to his feet. Voices continued to urge him on, celebrating his return. Others wept as well, for pity or from madness. He hadn't understood how much there was to miss until he felt the desire rising again. The weeping grew louder. *Christ,* listen *to them all, their prayers and cries.* How could he hope to ever put a stop to it? That part of his soul was growing outside himself, perhaps having lived much better than him, or perhaps only dying in the dirt; one half wanted the other back, like a mate whose touch he could no longer bear. The moon brushed through his hair. He had to put a stop to this *we need* of lovers tearing him into pieces again, then fumbling with what they found as they tried to put him back together. Bushes shook, and branches parted.

Something low and to his left called him Lucifer.

"Elizabeth," he said, for only she would understand, whoever she was. The name held power in his past. A girl with a red ribbon, and maybe that was his blood in the corner of her mouth.

Jacob dropped forward and passed out, breathing earth, as any number of eyes wept for him.

## *Chapter Six*

Kathleen Donleavy, usually called Katie except by the old Irishmen on Seventy-third Street, who liked to sing the song to her, their cancerous throats adding a heavy resonance to *Kathleeeeeeen*, looked in the rearview mirror again. She watched the black road unwinding behind her as though it were strewn with her shredded poetry, a copy of the *Isaac Maelstrom Trivia & Quiz Book*, her Philippines research paper she hadn't completed,

Grandma's glasses, and, of course, Tim and the baby.

"What's the matter?" Lisa asked.

"Nothing," Katie said.

"You've got that look again."

"I feel like I can't travel twenty minutes outside of the city without completely falling off the planet. We mapped it out; we had three different colored pens and dots and arrows showing us the way. We've got a compass bobbing on the dashboard—look at the stupid thing. How could we get so far off track?"

"For a map to be helpful in the least you have to have a reference point. I haven't seen a highway number or street sign or mile marker for the past half hour. And we're not that far off track; we're in the vicinity—it's just a matter of finding the right back roads. Don't worry about it."

"I'm not."

She wasn't. She'd been out of D wing of the hospital eleven weeks—what they'd called the Ding-a-ling wing—and usually felt about this close to going back in, but the past few days had been good ones. She was in motion, finally, thanks to Lisa, moving toward a sort of obsession perhaps, what with the *written* and the *writer* both meaning so much—maybe too much—but it was a direction and a goal.

It had been so long since she'd had any. She felt a touch more insecure but a little less depressed every mile of the trip.

"Well," Lisa said. "We're between Caracas, Venezuela, and Sukkertoppen, Greenland."

"At least we're not lost," Katie said.

Folding and unfolding the map with the multicolored arrows and dots, snapping it open and shut as if she were playing an accordion, Lisa finally threw it in the backseat. "All right, so I admit that I can't figure this damn thing out, but we're close by; I know that much. That island is really just a bunch of woods cut off from the rest by four rivers."

"Four rivers? Is that possible?"

"That's what it looks like on here, but who the hell knows?" Lisa peered through the passenger window at the pure darkness, the moon illuminating nothing, leaving nothing to see. "Not even eight o'clock and it's pitch-black out. Don't you think you're going a little fast?"

"No."

"I think you are, a bit."

Only because she kept hoping to get away from everything else coming after her from behind; yes, a bit, but still never fast enough. "I'm only doing forty-five."

"Forty-five around here can send us off a cliff or into a tree."

"Okay, I'll slow down."

"I mean, I know you're psyched about meeting the guy of your wildest literary fantasies; interviewing him will certainly be more fun than finding old Filipinos and asking them about the twenties."

Lisa liked to fall into grooves and run along the same track over and over. She got a big kick out of not having gone to college, secure in her employment and place in the world, and liked to rub Katie's nose into some of the more dumb core courses she'd had to take. "A lot of people have done their dissertations on his work; it would be intriguing to see what he has to say about it." If he said anything at all, or could explain to her just how you went on after something like that.

"Or is it the son of the man? Is he the one you like reading, or is it his father? I'm not sure."

Neither was Katie, really, but she had a suspicion. Every time she thought of what she was doing she wanted to sharply jar her brain with the heel of her hand; she couldn't believe it herself. Exactly what had happened to get her to go out and buy a compass and watch it swing by in floating degrees? A year and a half ago she'd been your average college student cruising through her sophomore year, with her own apartment, a part-time job at the university, and a live-in boyfriend, Timothy. How much more Norman Rockwell could you get than *Timothy?* . . . Frankie or Joey or Tommy made you think of wiseguys, and even John came across with too much of a biblical edge, but Timothy sounded as apple-pie and innocuous as Howdy Doody.

Maybe the cocaine habit wasn't so average, but it didn't affect anything at the time. Her own plan of a comfortable future as housewife and possible middle-class, local-paper columnist, talking about her kids, dogs, prices of minivans, and the vagaries of the PTA had abruptly been chucked, beginning with the baby.

She lowered the window to get some air while Lisa fidgeted with the CD player and put in something with a disco flavor. A heavy bass beat thrummed from the speakers, steadily filling the car. "Oh, hey, now, you can't be serious. From industrial to *Saturday Night Fever?*"

"Gotten a taste for some of the boogaloo lately."

"And I know his name."

Lisa grinned, but as usual when they spoke

67

of Robert Wakely, she hid a serious pout in there, a lot more going on than she would admit. "Quiet, you." The map lay unraveling across the backseat as if trying to open itself again. She reached back, pulling it forward, and drew it flat across her lap, using the dash light to find the green, orange, and blue course they'd set out for themselves.

"I think it's called boogie," Katie said, "not boogaloo."

"Oh, that's it; now I remember. Boogie. 'I love the night life; I love to boogie.' Thank you for clarifying that point."

"Sheesh, you nasty critter."

The baby had come and gone in only two months last year, leaving behind a trail of love and hate like nothing she'd ever dealt with before. Not long after had ensued a night of shouting and throwing fragile shower gifts against the wall, an ordeal that had progressed from a stupid slap fight into a cocaine-induced boxing match with Timothy that had landed her in the same hospital, although on a different floor. In the weeks following—as her jaw set and they'd both gotten some much-needed drug rehab—she'd realized he'd taken the loss of the child even harder than she had.

"Um . . . maybe we should go right here?"

Lisa said. A broad curve opened into a veering fork, neither lane looking particularly well traveled. Reflectors flashed against the rock face and a number of trees, the two unlit roads heading off in opposite directions.

"Okay."

"Don't agree so quickly; I have no idea."

"Then why'd you say it?"

"I wanted to give you all the options."

"So let's turn right."

"No," Lisa told her, smoothing the map against her thigh, her knees still a little bruised from Bob's hardwood floors. "Go straight."

"Okay."

Katie could still see that look in her mother's blue-contact-lensed brown eyes when she had found her daughter back on the doorstep with her luggage and a wired jaw. Katie thought that surviving that shattering gaze of disappointment was probably the most difficult moment of the entire year outside of flushing the fetus. And Lisa was talking abortion.

Timothy had gotten clean, found a new job that he enjoyed, and started going to counseling at a place run by ex-addicts who rode Harleys and had ponytails and didn't talk with insubstantial euphemisms like most of the therapists did. Katie had still held out a little hope that they might get together again; first they would recover themselves and then possibly each other. He held off from the cocaine and tequila, but the occasional beer got him working into the old mind-set again—an addict is an addict—and though the Harley guys kept waggling their scarred hands in his face, nothing could force change unless it happened on the inside. Before Tim had had time to ruin his life again he'd pinned his Mazda under a tractor-trailer hauling a few tons of potatoes, both of them doing in excess of sixty at three in the morning.

"You've got that face again," Lisa said.

"What is this face you keep talking about? You say it like there's somebody else in the car here."

Sometimes that was the way Lisa thought about it, too. She'd look up from the map and see this lady driving, and it would take her half a second to realize it was Katie with that face on. "Kind of pretty, actually; the guys will really go for it. Let me see if I can describe this lady. Eyebrows up high on your forehead, lips so flattened they pull your mouth down low, changing the angle of your jaw, but you still manage to squint a little. It makes you look like a hit woman out on a job."

"You know this for a fact? What social circles are you running in now, Lise? What kind of parties is Bobby taking you to out in Red Hook? Is he handling all the Gambino autobiographies now?"

"Oh, this is a nice disposition."

Katie let out a stale breath and tried to let the hinges of her jaw relax, to change the face back into her own. "I'm sorry. Look, I'm feeling a little freaked-out about this whole idea. I don't want him to think I'm a crazy fan. And I know it could make trouble for you, too."

"Let's just say I'm not too worried about what Bobby might think of me at the moment."

"Please don't say it like that. I don't want to cause problems for you two."

"You aren't. Besides, what's the worst thing Jacob can do to us? Not let us in the house?"

Or let them in. Both Maelstroms, father and son, had written more than their share of sensitive, erotically tender, occasionally schlock novels featuring flesh-ripping knife-kill scenes, to offer a thick body of classic terrifying fiction. So which of them pulled Katie forward? It had become magnetic in a way, horror drawn to horror. She felt like some groupie chasing a smeared-eyeliner rock band, or one of those soap-opera devotees who truly thinks the people on the screen cuddling together on channel four actually *are* lovers in life. She'd met a few of them in the hospital, who couldn't make the segue between television and life. Katie's own resistance to fantasy had been worn away the past couple of years. Her senior thesis on Camus' concept of man's expiation from God had been altered and refined, distilled, or maybe only corrupted into its present state of confused journalistic narrative. She had to find something that made a little sense.

Horror drawn to horror.

Who knew what kind of night this would be if they could ever find the place?

"Cute, you say . . . ?" she murmured.

Lisa pitched sideways and steadied herself against the back of the seat, wondering if the doctors were right in letting her best friend out of the Ding-a-ling wing so soon. Lisa didn't know if she was helping Katie through something or just setting her up for a greater fall. *God, let it be okay*. She looked down at the orange and blue arrows and seemed to get a sense of where they were heading. "Hey, keep your eyes on the road, and slow down; I think we're almost there."

# Chapter Seven

Darkness loomed over the keystones and ironwork trimming of the roof. A fathomless black bathed everything in a fashioned web of discreet and unkempt luster. The weather vane creaked faster. A slick sheen gliding off the house dispersed into the shadows of the forest as though trick-or-treating with neighborhood children.

Jacob hadn't been able to find the lantern again as he'd stumbled up the driveway. His head continued to sizzle, his eyes leaking something viscous that didn't feel like tears, giving the night a baleful blue gloss. Somehow the moon left him enough light to see his way to the front door. Exhausted from the struggle, still fighting to keep them out and yet keep them in, he wanted only to sleep.

If they would let him.

The gables were wounded eyes searching the land, and the bay windows confronted him with stained glass so perfect they begged to be broken, as if out of reverence for fragile human life. For each of the dead.

He had smashed them once, those panes.

With a wooden sword he'd hurled at his sister just as she was about to set her fangs into Joseph's corded neck. Dad was already dead by then, impaled about a quarter mile away; Mom had been rescued, hidden in the brush. His brother, immobile in his wheelchair and waiting on the porch, didn't care much at all, always irate and bored. Joseph sat paging through a literary journal, pages tearing in his hands as he occasionally looked up with unsheathed scorn and frustration, swatting flies hovering around his sweaty back. Of course, Rachel would try to get to him.

She proved to be sneaky, seriously into guerrilla warfare. She made the perfect succubus, switching characteristics off and on as she needed them, pulling text from their father's illustrated encyclopedia, *Demonic and Monstrous: A Guide to the Diabolical*. Rachel could become anyone with one slick line of lipstick and a swirl of rouge; everything inhuman could be beautiful in her hands, on that face.

Dad, her partner in these ventures, child of Baal, slave to Moloch the child-eater, enjoyed the mad dash through the woods and writing and rewriting their adventures as they played them out. Mother became Snow White under fire, Guinevere polished into sainthood, and Juliet on the balcony, the only woman in Jacob's world who would allow him to protect her.

So *Nosferachel* is making a wild break from the forest, sprinting for the porch, needing to tag Joseph to win; it's a mistake and everyone knows it. Their father wags his head and grins because Rachel is too impatient, and Jacob, although also impatient, manages to always outwait her.

Mom and Dad are both now sitting on a tree stump, watching the battle winding down after so many hours in the sun. Torn pages from the literary journal litter the area, wafting in the breeze. With features sculpted to perfection, Joseph stares at his siblings with a practiced sneer of abhorrence. It's been a long game today, and it makes absolutely no difference to him who wins and who dies; he's still a cripple. The family has urged him to join in and play along, but their endless patronizing habits humiliate him. He is the Maltese Falcon, the golden idol of Pago-Pago, the grand prize, and home base. He cannot die.

Jacob could have told them just when Rachel was going to make a run for it—he can feel her nerves grating, the anxiety mashing up against her like the hands of boys at her old school. He crawls from the bushes and sees that although he has the advantage and remains in the better position, his sister's sixteen-year-old legs are already pumping her out of his reach. Her laughter is a dark and enigmatic charm. Her stride is longer than his, and if he doesn't press himself for all he's worth, she's going to win. The fangs leave soft white indentations against her lower lip. She's tucked her cape into her waistband so it won't slow her down. At the most he's got maybe five seconds before she rips past him. He moves on a collision course, giggling nervously.

" 'You won't get away, witch!' " he says.

" 'The green wood of the stake is too fresh for you!' " It's from one of their father's earliest stories, one of his favorites about the warlock hunter McNellis of Ariovagne, but Rachel plays for keeps and doesn't waste breath on that kind of fun. Four seconds left, and now she's got so much momentum that even if he could get in front of her she'd just bowl him over. She'd do it, too; she'd bring the heel of her fist against his jaw, kick him, do whatever it took. If he drops the sword she can kill him, and even though she's never tried before, he's hesitant. There's something grotesque in the curl of her clown lips today. Two seconds, and he knows he's lost her; Joseph's going to get those curved incisors clamped onto him, and he's grinning up there like a king on the ruby throne, looking joyfully anxious and squeamish.

"No!" Jacob howls. The errant knight, despite his human weaknesses, can't lose to such demons. Running, he hauls his arm back and swings the sword out sideways at her just as Rachel hits the first step of the porch. The wooden sword heaves like a boomerang, whipping in a hideous arc toward her head. He imagines her brains leaking out of her ears, cape writhing in the wind, her breasts heaving with a staggered breath in their brother's arms. He shrieks and tries to recall the moment. For an instant it feels as if he's actually done so, reeling back his own insane actions—the edges of his vision flicker, and he sees himself, or someone who appears to be him, standing inside the house staring out through the window.

She reaches Joseph, and he sights the whirling weapon over her shoulder as she leans forward with that wild smile, tittering now, and with a flick of her tongue lunges for his throat. He gasps, from her lips or the threat, and sort of smiles. With those powerful arms he heaves her flopping across his lap just as the plank brushes past her ear and smashes the bay windows.

His mother and father, now moving to him, are too stunned to say anything. He checks their faces, spotting some disillusion and disappointment—but not even much of that—all of them too busy with the complexities of design. Everyone analyzes their own portion of the greater whole, too self-absorbed to act, not caring much about anything except how this new chemistry between them fits into much grander, more personal schemes.

Rachel pushes off their brother's chest, stands with arms raised victoriously, and gives Jacob a smirk that digs deeper because of its meaninglessness. Dad laughs an unrestrained laugh that shifts into a girlish giggle, and the sound is so unfamiliar that Jacob winces. Heavy fragments of glass plink off the windowsill and drop into the flower beds.

Mom pulls at the screen door, holding it open wide enough for his brother to roll inside, then lets it swing shut as they proceed to the left, away from the litter of shards on the floor, and he hears her asking his brother to help with folding the laundry. Such lack of temper, it doesn't make sense. Dad ruffles Jacob's hair and heads off to putter around in the garage. Rachel bobs her ponytail in his direction, doing a slow dance as she unwinds herself from the cape, showing good faith between winner and loser in this game, and gives him an unprovoked hug of either hatred or forgiveness. His breath comes in bites, all of them leaving him, fading out as he reflects on this murder he's nearly committed, seeing her skull cracked open and leaking into Joseph's lap.

He walks inside and averts his eyes as he passes the dining room; the breeze from the new hole hisses platitudes of regret. He shrugs off the wind, goes up to his room, and lies on the bed, guilt swarming as the tears catch on his tongue. The edges of his vision still flicker, bright white with threads of crimson in it, as if there is blood hanging on the walls.

Won't they punish him . . . ?

Exhausted from the struggle, fighting to keep them out and yet keep them in, he wanted only to sleep.

If they would let him.

Jacob stumbled toward the house, standing directly on that spot of the porch where his brother had drawn Rachel to safety. There was power in such events, where the past could pull you backward. Something small but alive near his foot crawled across the step. A turtle glared at him. He brought his hand to the stained glass, scratched at it as if it might purr, and tried to remember who'd found the sword on the carpet, who had replaced the panes, and what had happened after that.

He pulled the key to the front door from his pocket, and felt no surprise that it still fit perfectly. After all these years of renting the house to other authors—respected associates of his father who wrote tributes to the man by ripping off his plots and doing second-rate jobs at quasi sequels—not one had so much as scratched the doorknob. The tumblers moved as easily as liquid, and with barely a nudge the hand-carved oak door brushed back with a draft of musty air. He sensed more than saw that none of the writers had inflicted their own wills upon the decorum, none of the furniture had been touched, nothing taken, nothing left behind. He could make out some sheets that had been tossed haphazardly over a few tables, a chair, the grandfather clock. For reasons either aesthetic, atmospheric, or perhaps even practical, a commandment had been held to the house: Do not disturb.

Nearly all of them went on to complete relatively popular novels, though none stayed here for more than a few months. The house had been vacant now for nearly a year. Their publishing successes were a fact no book reviewer overlooked, this gift from the maelstrom—they liked to throw in the drama as much as they could, playing with analogies, pointing out that this had been an ambience in which the Maelstroms died, but others had found their greatest success.

He shut the door and walked into the ebony envelope of his home again, drifting in the maddening circles of the rooms, hoping to find some reason for this labyrinth of history and memory. He picked up his pace, heading for the stairway, no longer thinking about going to the basement to hit the circuit breakers and turn on the lights, not caring about human fears or foibles now.

"Beth?" he whispered. "Beth, I need you."

And he knew where he would find her, of course. In the same place where she'd always resided, staring out from behind his winter clothes.

Upstairs. In his bedroom.

In the closet.

# *Chapter Eight*

The moon's glow glinted off the scarce leaves and dappled Katie's eyes with silver-etched sight. After five hours behind the wheel she was too tired to drive anymore, and at Lisa's frantic insistence they had pulled over to rest while they were in the area, before they went into a river or a ravine.

Lisa lay in the backseat with her coat spread under her, legs kicked up against the window, tapping her feet in a quirky disco

beat although they'd turned off the music.
From her prone position in the front Katie
could make out the cracked polish on Lisa's
toenails reflecting with a faint, shining white.

"You sleeping?" she asked.

"No. This seat belt's breaking my back."

"Me, too." A pause lengthened, the milieu
between them thickening. It amazed her how
little they'd spoken during the trip, each of
them so comfortable in the silence. It worried
her. "Thanks for going along with me on this
nutty scheme."

"I think it's pretty interesting. Or will be if
you actually get to write a book about him. If
nothing else, maybe you can write a Jacob
Maelstrom quiz book. Bob would probably
love to do something like that. The other one
sold really well, from what he tells me."

"How'd you get him to open up and give
you the address?"

"I didn't. After screwing around last night,
I rummaged through his e-mail address book
and took some of the names you gave me of
the authors who wrote books in this place. A
couple of them had their snail mail addresses
cross-referenced with Stonethrow Island."

"Pretty good, Mata Hari."

No, she'd fouled up, and was becoming
more certain of the fact. "You think we

should have called them and asked for directions?"

"I think they all realize that their writing novels in that house was really just a publicity scam and they couldn't help but have their books compared unfavorably to Isaac Maelstrom's work."

There it was again in the way she said that silly name, Maelstrom—*shit, talk about a publicity scam*—with Katie throwing so much into it, saying "Isaac Maelstrom" with a whispery hiss, like a worshiper of ancient idols. As if everyone in the world ought to be impressed and glorify someone who just wrote about killers, monsters, and girls who yacked up pea soup. Katie's eyes dimmed. It reminded Lisa of the Jews who refused to write the word *God* in their articles, and even spelled out *g\*d*, as if He were always watching and reading the newspapers, and would come down from heaven and slap them around if they didn't put in the asterisk.

"Was the guy really that good?" Lisa asked.

Katie thought about how she should explain it to someone who had never read a complete novel and found nothing extraordinary in words. Lisa knew how to make an entire room turn when she entered, how long to stay and exactly when to leave, and how to always make the world work for her no matter how alone she might ever find herself, but she could never understand the significance of poetry. "He had the tail of something that nobody else had grabbed before. His writing itself varied from brilliant to downright awful . . . so does Jacob's. Some think that their inconsistency is part of their charm, but I think it goes deeper than that. Either way, they both have the unnameable quality that separates the unique from the common."

Hearing Katie talk with such reverence almost scared Lisa—nobody outside of a fanatic should become so breathless when they spoke—but more than anything, as they waited lost in the woods when she ought to be at Bob's beach house with him, it bored her. "Listen, it's only a little before nine, but you're wiped; I can hear it in your voice." She kicked down the armrest so they could see more of each other. "You should have split the driving with me." Lighting a cigarette, she took a long drag and gave it to Katie, who only puffed tentatively, as though fearing it was a joint and would start her down the whole long trip again, and quickly handed it back.

Lisa smoked too much lately, heading into two packs a day, as if daring the kid to live through the haze of fumes she'd force it to breathe.

"You sound like it, too," Katie said.

"What?"

"Wiped. Are you all right?"

"Yes."

Another silence, deeper this time but not as meaningful as Katie hoped for. She wished one of them would just snap and get the whole thing rolling. There had been an argument roiling beneath all that they'd said to each other for months. It seemed both of them had their jealousies, reservations, and uncertainties, maybe even about each other.

After a few seconds more of heavy quiet came an abrupt noise, small but like a gunshot in the stillness. They both sat up. Something had begun *shifting* in the woods, as though unwinding to a better position, jaws jutting, some kind of claw reaching forward under the car.

"Did you hear that, Lise?"

"Of course I heard. Don't say it like that. It's just an animal; relax."

"Yes, but—"

"Look, Katie—"

"I'm just trying to say that—"

"I know what you're trying to say, but—"

"Lise, would you let me finish a sentence?"

"No, quit freaking out or—"

They'd been chafing each other for a while now; it was only a matter of time before it blew up into something more serious. Whatever had shifted and unwound fell quiet. In the distance, they could just make out the subtle strains of rivers sounding, creeping through the night, making them both feel like fools for coming this close but not being able to find the damn bridge. After another strained minute without follow-up they settled back.

"So . . ." Katie said.

Lisa had only an instant to decide which tack to take, unveiling or interrogation. "So you ever going to tell me exactly what we're trying to prove by coming here after him?"

Slick move, with her turning the tide like that. Maybe the ball couldn't just come on out and get rolling; they had to figure out which stances to take first, decide what they could get away with bringing up and what they couldn't. It got tricky at times, especially this answer. "I don't know what you're doing here on this crazy ride, but I'm working on my thesis."

"This isn't your thesis."

"It is, but that's not the only reason. You would have been better off going to Bobby's beach house with him when he asked you to."

"You think I'd just let you come out here on your own, walk up to him without a formal word of introduction?"

"You met him for ninety seconds."

True enough, but he appeared to know how to handle Bob, and she needed to ask him a little about that. "It was time Bobby and I got a few days away from each other in order to relax. He's been on edge lately, and I have been, too. It hasn't been all his fault, and I don't want it all to burn out when it's barely begun." She kept tapping to the disco, the soles of her feet moving along the window in a weird kind of box step. *One, two, three; one, two, three.* "Besides, it's too damn cold at the shore."

Okay, they'd leave it at that for a while, skirting the main issues but at least having them on hand in case anybody wanted to come back and dip into them later. Katie understood how insecure Lisa felt in her attachments, not wanting to be the hot trailer-park tramp after the older guy only for his wallet, but realizing the money and thirtieth-floor apartment held a crucial status in the world, especially New York. She wondered if Lisa could really go through with an abortion or whether there'd be a strenuous push for marriage, and if that would bring them down even harder.

"What did you tell him?" Katie asked. "About where you were going this weekend."

"That your sister just had a baby girl, and we were going to spend some time with her."

"My sister didn't just have a baby."

"Yes," Lisa said. "Hold on, I recall that now."

"I don't have a sister."

"Yes, it's all becoming clear."

Despite the quibbles and qualms that harbored deeper ills, Katie felt a flood of gratitude. Lisa didn't know about Grandma and Grandpa and the knives that cut leather, and yet she'd willingly been drawn into this excursion. Maybe she went along solely out of friendship, or maybe she simply wanted to question Jacob at length about what kind of man Robert Wakely was, what kind of man the father of her baby was—either way, Lisa had stood by her through these last demented months, and Katie already owed her more than she could ever say. "Thanks, Lise. Listen . . . listen, I want you to understand how much I appreciate all that you've done for me, and for coming along." It became sappy and stilted when she said it out loud.

"You think I would've missed this?"

"Of course you would've."

"No way, we needed some adventure."

"Okay," Katie said.

Lisa thought about it for a second. Of course she would've. She hated lying to Bob about the baby and all this other shit, but there was nothing else to do. Katie's last restrung nerves were near snapping again; she looked worse than when she went into the hospital the last time, with the dark circles around her eyes like when Tim used to backhand her into the bookcase. So she had to look out for her best friend, put in a little overtime here, like she didn't have enough on her mind. *Let's just put that aside for the moment.* Forget the pro-lifers; even the abortion clinic folks themselves looked at her as though she were a homicidal maniac, even when she was only there to pick up some papers, checking out her options. Jesus, they all wanted to kill somebody.

The thesis thing was bullshit; Katie needed to get in on the whole survivor gig, and saw something she could sympathize with in an eleven-year-old Jacob Maelstrom who'd lived through butchery. She wanted to find out how the man had handled the past outside his fiction. There were sharper edges to that kind of reasoning, ones equally cutting, in the same way Bob had started acting this past week, unstable and a little mean, everybody with their secrets starting to spill out.

Lisa had quizzed one of the reporters who'd called the office looking to interview Jacob, but she'd been only halfheartedly interested in his responses, really, despite the commotion lately. She'd never read any of their books and never would. She hadn't read Bob's either, but had looked at the photos of the whited-out bodies on the floor. She figured that Jacob was deeply ill inside because almost everyone was, so it made sense. She knew only the basic story of what had happened, none of the particulars that Katie had become so obsessed with, the fascination creeping into her eyes like a syrupy poison. Lisa wondered if this was Katie's way of working up to suicide. "So what's the whole story on him, huh? About this weekend. About this murder."

"Multiple murders."

"What happened?"

"Didn't you read Bob's books?"

"No."

"You know any of the details?"

"No. And Bob shies away from the publicity. He's been squirrely lately, even at home. I'm under strict orders to just slam the phone down on anyone after information, and I guess I'm trying hard not to learn anything about it."

"Uh-huh."

So Lisa was going to make Katie talk it out, like the counselors who sat there just staring at you, asking you questions about everything you could imagine: why you brushed your teeth the way you did, what you thought about your breasts, if you masturbated with perishables, when was the last time you had your head checked for lice, and about Grandpa. How could Lisa not know anything about the most celebrated clients at the agency she worked for, one of the truly notorious crimes of all time, with three books written by her own lover and more still coming out every few years? And what reasons could Robert Wakely have to kill all publicity? An agent turning them away? *Couldn't be.*

"Isaac Maelstrom, Jacob's father, moved up here to get out of the city grind and devote more time to his work and family."

"This is a fact?"

"What?"

"You say it like it's a fact. Devote time to his work and family, that sounds like jacket copy to me. You sure that was the reason?"

A deliberate slash—it sounded like Lisa

wanted to dig in a little in order to see if Katie really knew what she was talking about. "He and his wife had three kids. Joseph, the oldest, was a cripple, then Rachel, a couple of years younger, and Jacob, five or six years younger than her. Maelstrom wrote eleven novels here, had a cult following that grew steadily until he became a best-seller."

"Okay, I'm with you. Now there's a *then* coming."

"Sure. Then, for no reason anyone's discovered, when she was seventeen Rachel locked Jacob in his bedroom closet and killed the rest of the family with an ax, hacking off their heads and hiding them." Amazing how commonplace it sounded, not quite as bad as the Empire State Building massacre or the latest guy who went postal in McDonald's. "No one ever found them."

"You're fucking with me."

"No. She finally decapitated herself by bracing the blade at the top of the stairs and dropping her neck forward onto it. Front door was open; police figured her own head rolled down the steps and was taken by an animal."

"Hold it, wait a second. . . ." Lisa tried to hold on to that thought for more than a moment, and couldn't do it. "They never found her head either? Is that what you're saying? An animal took it, is that what you just told me? Like a muskrat goes looking for a person's head, takes it home, and drops it in a burrow someplace?" She shrugged and nearly laughed. "How the hell can that be? It's impossible."

"It's insane, but not impossible. A few days later Wakely found them, with Jacob dehydrated and nearly dead by then. He said he had no idea why she did it, and nobody ever found out anything more. I thought you knew some of this."

"No." The cigarette had burned down almost to her fingers. She stubbed it out on the car mat, realizing she didn't know what she'd gotten into. "Bobby never said a word about any of that. I suppose he expected me to have known it already." Or never wanted to mention it again—walking into a house splashed full of blood, missing heads, a muskrat staring at a neck? She thought about his occasional moans in the night, kicking under the covers. Did he keep going back? "It makes a lot more sense to me that somebody else got in the house and killed them, no?"

"Made sense to the cops, too, but forensics showed that she did it all herself."

"Maybe with a partner?"

Katie gave a noncommittal nod. "Why do you think people are still writing about it? Because there's so much speculation, some really ridiculous theories."

"I can imagine." She suddenly felt extremely foolish for having brought Katie here, as if she'd initiated them into what could be embarrassing, absurd, or emotionally dangerous for somebody. "And you want to ask this guy about his family being killed like that? You expect him to open up about what it was like? You're going to interview him?"

"I don't know what I expect." Maybe she felt a kinship to the type of curdling he must've suffered; she could feel more parts of him dying with each new novel: his aspirations failing, his resistance weakening. Lisa mentioned he'd been quiet and polite, but Katie could only see him with his head flung back, screaming, but his voice too weak to be heard, and growing fainter each time out. Perhaps she could help him find the words he couldn't grasp anymore, talking to him, chatting instead of questioning, holding him for a while if it didn't seem too insane. Maybe he would know something about leather and knives.

Lisa snorted, almost glad they couldn't get there. "You're not going to . . . ?"

"To what, Lise? Act like a crazy fan, like your Aunt Frieda, who thinks statues of the Virgin Mary wink at her? Listen, you're beautiful; you don't—"

"Oh, please."

" 'Oh, please' yourself." Katie fought to keep the tears out of her throat. "You've gone up against the odds and come through the whole haul on your own, with no one but yourself to rely on. For you there's nobody else to blame when something doesn't go right in your life, never anybody under your nose who might . . ."

Lisa tightened, feeling an echo of morning sickness, understanding she'd started this herself; she never should have taken jabs at Katie. "Look, I'm sorry."

It was hopeless to put it into words when talking to someone who didn't know the meaning of those words. How could Lisa understand being self-conscious, consumption by fear? She was going to hit the abortion clinic next week; how do you talk about the terror of losing a baby and a lover to someone like that? But with Jacob Maelstrom you wouldn't have to explain anything, just make sense of the sentences, try to bleed off some of his guilt. She desired his weaknesses to complement her own.

"No, I'm sorry, Lise. You've been great and I've been nothing much besides a burden."

"I love you and will stick by you, you know."

"I do know."

Music of the rivers running, as if the car were underwater. Wind rose, trees shaking across the moonlight, tossing shadows against the hood. Clouds roiled in the sky, a storm brewing in the mountains.

"I hope we don't run into any *Deliverance* types up here, some muskrat with a collection of skulls."

"We won't."

Again with the facts, Katie sounding too certain, without a hint of the insecurity or confusion she usually dragged around.

Get the fuck out of here, Lisa thought. Because no matter what, you had to wonder: so who took her head?

## Chapter Nine

Cobwebs and dust had grown thick in his bedroom; water stains in the high corners now stretched across to the center of the ceiling, making faces, posturing, even spelling out his nightmares in a runny cursive. Some words were printed, block letters, but other script ran over her sentences, denying him answers.

He'd found blankets in the linen closet down the hall, new sheets with little ducks on them, and another set with geese. He couldn't remember which tenant had a thing for birds; one of them had written a horror novel called *These Crimson Wings where Flies Hell*. A lot of mothballs were scattered around, but the odor wasn't nearly strong enough to overpower the scent of his mother's lilies.

Pillows propped behind his neck, Jacob pulled the covers up to his throat, the moon wafting in just enough for him to make out the changing text on the walls and ceiling. They were like page proofs handed to him for correction, to go over one more time before they saw final print. His blazing headache had dulled to a strange cadence outside of himself, as if it had no connection to his pulse.

On the verge of sleep, lying in his own bed again, he stared into the closet where Rachel had kept him.

He watched as color swam behind the crack, a hint of pink, like lips pressed to the jamb, and heard Beth say, "I love you."

Darkness paled, yielding, as the door shuddered and slowly opened. A section of night folded back unevenly, like a dog-eared page of a well-read book. His bedroom heaved with sudden illumination: yellow with a splash of red so bright that if he'd been fully awake he would've had to squint. Words crawled down the walls to settle on his face, sliding down his throat. The door slammed shut as if yanked closed from the other side. Tides of his father's ink flooded around the bed once more, black tendrils trailing over the covers, weaving between his fingers, and sluicing into his nostrils. The weather vane on the roof clanged and spun faster as the storm gathered, curtains billowing over his face now, the window raised a few inches. A soft patter of drizzle began, leaking onto the sill and dripping over.

Someone quietly spoke words in his room. He strained to hear if it was himself, or another. The door eased open again, as if more cautious. Yellow, with a spot of red, an outline framed in there gesturing to him on the bed. Rising wind violently tore at him beneath the sheets as an eruption of rain pounded against the glass, spraying his forehead. In a few minutes water began rippling through the ceiling, adding new paragraphs of stains to be read.

In that saffron dress, with her chestnut hair drawn slightly to one side and affixed with a cherry bow, Elizabeth stood before him. She'd always been here, clothed like this, surrounded with an aura of the summer solstice, wild roses, scarecrow hay, and honey. She'd aged with him. *You either are a little-girl ghost or you aren't; you either came back from the dead to teach a lonely boy about love or you didn't.* Twenty-one years old now, mirroring himself, and he could see she was ill. Her face's normal rose complexion had been suffused with wrinkles of strain, dark, sagging flesh dangling below her eyes. She'd told Wakely she was dying.

Jacob caressed her shoulders, kissing her bottom lip and drawing it into his mouth, nibbling. He almost felt like one of the guys in the park, lying on a blanket with his arm around his sweetheart. Part of him got out of bed; a portion remained sleeping there. Still, he could think of no one more beautiful. She had always been everything he could never bear to be without, yet had been without all these years. He'd never been able to love anyone else. A sob broke from his cracked heart, and ill as she'd become it was Elizabeth who held him now. Jacob dropped to his knees, and she tumbled beside him until they embraced on the floor.

On the bed, he snorted, dreaming.

He had promises to keep

She smiled, healthier perhaps, and lifted his palm to her lips. "Don't be afraid."

"I'm not."

"It's been so long."

"Yes . . ."

"Too long, my liege."

It caught him low in the belly, that title, like sharpened fingernails digging for meat.

With a gasp Jacob froze, hearing the familiar name, whatever it had been and continued to be, she had no right to call him that. Only the muses knew him as *liege*—and the haze swirled and thinned, veils twirling so that he caught glimpses of them here and there. He focused on her dress and what memories it forced into him, trying desperately not to stare at her sickness. *The muses, yes.*

He grappled sideways with his thoughts, rain on his face thinning the ink so that it ran down his neck, outlining his jugular. The soaked covers grew heavier as thunder raged and shook the house. He regained lost ground, concentrating on the freckles peppering her nose, her soft cheeks so different from the skin of snakes, and moaned as the storm tried to drive him awake.

"Don't ever call me that, Beth."

"But, my love—"

"Don't do it. It can't be that way." Her smile dropped to a sorrowful grin as she brought her hand to his throat, her nails tracing the veins ticking in his neck. He fanned her hair over her shoulders, as far as the tight red bow would permit. "I just want to hold you."

"That's enough for the moment then, so long as I am with you, love. Let me touch you, Jacob."

"God, yes."

Breathing in his ear, taking the same breaths he did, she slid to his side and soon fell everywhere around him. It all seemed to pass instantly, time distorted by the *need*. The present teetered, and he saw himself again as a child, playing Monopoly on the floor with Joseph rolling forward, leaving tire tracks of blood. He became too much of himself, as if others scratched at him from the inside, biting and scrabbling, trying to find release through his eyes and pores.

His mother's words ran down out of the wall, followed by his father's, flowing together until he couldn't read any of it. Beth licked his chin and kept whispering, and he didn't know why. They reached out and clasped, tickled, scratched and bit and fondled. Under the covers he sighed and shifted, unwinding in the shadows. Jacob felt more alive than he had in a decade.

She whispered, "Liege," and he wanted to die

*Master of many.*

*I am Legion, for we are many.*

A voice then, from under the mattress, where he began to thrash with the rain in his face. *Glad you could make it, Third.*

He mumbled in his sleep. "What's it all about, Rache?"

That part of him in the closet shambled forward to stand guard over Elizabeth. He shielded her, and had no idea against which of the dead—or all of them.

*You owe us*, his sister said, and he'd never heard anything spoken with that kind of glee. She could lunge into spots that nobody else had ever been able to reach; he'd gone through his life without ever feeling that much want or rage again. He'd been paying his price for years; what more could she possibly want from him? He backed up farther into the closet, and sinking lower into the wet bed as Beth moved against him, pulling at his arm as if about to flee with him. And where would they go? The house rumbled insanely.

Rachel moved then, grinning and clambering out from beneath the mattress, crawling through the dust, up the duck-covered sheets toward him. *Quack, quack.* She knelt there at the foot of the bed, and languidly the dead rose to encompass him, dragging her nails up to his throat and making a slicing motion across it. *Come dance with me, little brother.*

"No, never again," he said in her arms, feeling her body on his as she smeared herself against him, where she belonged.

Beth wept, hoping to hold him back.

He heard his father's typewriter.

# Chapter Ten

Fatigue can get you like this, opening the well of your unconscious and spraying out all the restless fugue and literary, little-girl fantasies. She circled to her right, then over to the left, onto her belly, like having sex with Tim again, who was always so big on different positions every few minutes. Pins and needles jabbed her feet, vestiges of menstrual cramps kept up a dull ache, and that nasty rubbing of the ersatz leather seat crunching under her ass was leaving a welt.

Funny how even in the hospital, in the middle of the constant muttering and occasional shouts and shrieks, with ladies licking the walls and sometimes each other, and fat chicks getting 2 A.M. enemas, she'd never had any trouble sleeping.

Sounds of the river arguing over boulders, and her stomach grumbling with a hapless voice kept her whirling in the front seat. She felt an almost human tugging at her midriff, as if the baby were still there. It demanded she roll to yet one more uncomfortable position, followed by twinges in her back from the sadistic safety belt. Collective minuscule hammers of rain now wailed down on the hood as though all the Chinese who'd ever lived were practicing their clever water tortures at once.

And at this second a mean brand of lightning fired the sky, as if searching someone out.

She had implicit trust in those nearly nonexistent blond baby hairs at the base of her neck; standing wiry and stiff they hit the primordial panic button. She had faith in her instincts, especially in the woods. Katie was sure, or nearly sure, that something waited, watching the car.

Okay, she knew she had to take charge of this expedition, instead of relying on Lisa to pull everything together for her all the time. Screw this sitting around, Katie thought as she started the car and hit the windshield wipers. How ridiculous to come this far and pull over on the side of the road, where they were bound to either get stuck in the mud or washed into the river.

Lisa shot up in the backseat, brushed the indents of her eyes, and said, "You can't see a thing in this rain."

"Onward," Katie said.

Crawling over the armrest into the passenger seat, Lisa shook her head, her scarlet hair turning to bloodshed in the reflection and refraction of the headlights striking the sheets of rain and the slippery tree trunks all around. She looked ecstatic to be moving again. "We're still lost."

"Nah."

As Katie began pulling back onto the road, the tires slid along the carpet of flooded grass and leaves, churning uselessly for a time before finally catching some traction. The front fender hit a branch, and the car slowly fishtailed into the thickening mush of the dirt road. She calmly steered into the skid until the tires bit and gripped and held.

"We're dead."

"No, see," Katie said, "we've simply ridden the circuitous route. Taken in the scenes, these real fine country sights, stopped to smell a few roses along the way like we're supposed to, Lise."

"Oh. That's what it was."

"Yes, see, we're there . . . we're right there."

Lisa shot her the usual glance, never sure of exactly when the men in the white coats should come running out with their butterfly nets, or whether they would nab *her* instead. "And how do you know that?"

"Because I finally figured out what went wrong. See, we have failed to consider the ruling hand of poetic justice." She sounded frantic, maybe high, but it just felt so good to be moving again. "We fell too easily before the steel fist of irony!" One arm was upraised, her index nail digging into the roof as if she were prodding God. "Never!"

"Kathleen, I think—"

"Repeat it, would you?"

She frowned. "Never. Okay?"

"Put some oomph into it!"

"Never! Oomph!"

Lightning skirted through the tousled trees,

making wild dashes among the rocks. Spear shafts of brilliance ripped into a million directions at once. Unknown languages carved into the darkness, written with a finesse of white fire. You could believe in myths out here. Legends came to life, the things they taught you in Catholic school, Cecil B. De-Mille movies; you could almost see Samson shouldering through the middle pillars in the cathedral of Dagon. Tree limbs shuddered, the woods moving with great sweeping motions around them, and the thunder seemed to erupt on top of the car.

Lisa gasped.

Katie's hands were trembling a little, and that wasn't a good sign by any means. She tried to keep the soundtrack of *Saturday Night Fever* out of her head, but the high-pitched harmony kept at her. She peered through the window as though waiting to apologize to the night, and talked faster to keep her mind off of everything else. "Think about it. Here we are, driving around for hours, blazing on trails Lewis and Clark would have balked at, looking for this bridge we know is supposed to be right here, right under our noses. Then we get tired and park out in the dark like inexperienced kids working with their first condom."

Lisa didn't know what to say, so she told the truth. "I'm still not all that good with them."

"So think about it for a moment, about our type of luck, and then ponder and weigh our good fortune against some of God's dirtier tricks."

Lisa thought about it, about all of it, especially how manic Katie sounded at this point, full of bravado but not necessarily false bravado. She didn't like when Katie talked about God; it meant she was feeling mystical. "Okay, I've pondered our predicament and decided we probably stopped one minute too soon, so the bridge ought to be right around the next curve." It might even be true.

"Exactly," Katie said, as they approached a narrow turn off that snaked into the forest; this had to be it, because that was the only way the world worked sometimes. She had to find the humor in fate and fear, and the surging knowledge that she had brought these events upon herself.

They still couldn't see the bridge. Riverwater frothed and churned beside them, their headlights showing nothing but fury. Lisa wiped precipitation off the inside of the windshield but still couldn't tell where they were heading. She rolled down the window and guarded her eyes against the driving rain.

"Was I right?" Katie asked. "Is it there?"

Lisa said, "It's there, but there's no way we're going over it."

Made of blocks of slick mortar and substantial wood, the bridge appeared to be hunkered like a toad, waves violently smashing against it. Katie pressed her foot down on the gas pedal moderately to keep from spinning down either side of the rocky bank, easing the car up to the base of the bridge. She felt like a gunslinger walking into town, marching with the *ching-ching* of her spurs resounding as the townsfolk came out to see what would happen when she drew.

From this angle the bridge looked more like a tunnel—the arching foam washing over its face made it appear as though a canopy covered the slimy stone.

"You see anything?"

"No. You sure this is the only way? Maybe there's like a real bridge somewhere, or a ferry."

"You're the one who got the directions, Lise. Did they say anything about a ferry?"

Stonethrow Island, right there, packed tightly inside the wall of dark but not a tangible fact yet. Katie tapped the steering wheel anxiously. Electron-moist earth called down more lightning to the vicinity, like a child gripping a yellow crayon to furiously slash against paper. The expanded air fell back, crushing the vacuum shut, and the car rocked to thunder. Branches scraped the roof, bushes gesturing—the townsfolk in need of a sheriff telling her to come on and shoot the sucker out of his socks already.

"What the hell do we do?" Lisa asked.

"Have some faith."

"I had lots of faith earlier, believe me. Not quite so much now, with God playing all those dirty tricks."

Filled with plenty of her own trepidation, Katie sighed, knowing they were pushing their limited luck, but how often did someone get to play at Alice like this? Adventures in the looking glass; except the glass was actually looking into her. The reality would never live up to this kind of funhouse ride; he'd probably slam the door in their faces. Even if he was kind enough to pity her fandom fanaticism, he'd never answer real questions, and she couldn't blame him for that. She'd never answered any either.

Beating out a crazed tattoo on the dashboard with her fingers now, Katie had to resuscitate her own faith. Something proved so tempting here. It seemed to be less dangerous rolling toward something than floating directionless, better to move than just lie in bed with your head full of shame and guilt.

Lisa grimaced, squinting, giving it a little too much Dirty Harry, but her gaze was set. "Are we going to try it?"

"I was thinking so."

"Fuck it, then; anything is better than just sitting here."

"My sentiments exactly." Katie threw the car into drive, watching the woods watching her.

The storm changed suddenly. That same kind of shifting, *unwinding*, out there in the dark—like a claw or hand gesturing, waving them on. She rubbed her eyes and drew her bangs clear, cold sweat exploding along her shoulders and neck. Features skirted in the bushes. She could almost see her grandmother's dentures propped on the old woman's chin, that shine on the edge of their porcelain bathtub. She could catch them glaring from the woods if she tried hard enough: faces of Nana's statues, all the martyred saints, shadows depicting various contortions of Christ, staring down at the scene on the slippery floor. For a moment the rain seemed to stop driving against the windshield, and moonlight appeared in strange patches, as if the storm had completely cleared and they sat outside on a different spring night. There was a little howl of air creeping in through the busted vent. Then the clamoring bellow again, of the downpour and river pounding, but not as wildly as her heart.

"You feel that?"

"What?"

"That," was all Katie could say. "That. Feel it?"

"No. The brakes?"

Headlights slipped over the brush and sludgy borders of the bridge, moving steadily into the surging torrent breaking over the stone. "What the hell . . . ?" She gunned it for a second, and there was an abrupt deluge of water sluicing over the hood, slamming the windshield, as the car rolled on with the vent wailing.

The pinging on the roof sounded like a typewriter clattering.

At last, escape from the envelope. They broke from the tide, rain receding back to a dull patter, and they simply drifted onto another muddy road. Lisa said, "I never liked sitting through a car wash, either."

Anxiety snapped with a nearly audible twang. The mood lightened immediately. Katie tittered, and the sound was so unnatural that Lisa giggled at her, making an even more uncharacteristic noise. They both groaned and dropped into nervous laughter, and checked about themselves, expecting more, taking turns looking in the rearview mirror, each thinking as their adrenaline leaked away, *That's it? Where's the nail-biting drama in that?*

Rain pummeled the surface tension of the pond, churning it into a bubbling, green froth. As the car splashed through the curves ahead, the lights kept catching on different kinds of movement: stirred up, yet with an odd effect toward the center—a slow, circular drawing motion.

Lisa casually glanced over, then away. "Okay, if we were fishing enthusiasts we'd know where to go."

Another few minutes and they saw the mansion. Katie tried to find a metaphor that fit, but couldn't quite pull it off. Nothing could do adequate justice to the vista opening before them. This was the charnel house of the Maelstroms. Butchery could be done anywhere, Katie knew, but few places could look like atrocity even from the outside, at night, a decade after.

Drowned moonlight and lightning gave her only a charcoal sketch of the house, the col-

onnades silhouetted against the hazy sky.
Windows were everywhere, some in high-
standing patterns, others octagonal and
stained-glass trapezoids. *So weird*. Walls ran
up into the roof, shingles and clapboards
knotted together, architectural styles rapidly
changing almost from foot to foot, first floor
to second to third. Strange angles played into
those gables that could be discerned. Across
the third story, settling backward against the
contrasting dormers, there seemed to be columns, porticos of some sort. She imagined
that up at the top stood an attic remade into
a den: the writing room.

"Like Salvador Dalí tried his hand at car-
pentry for a while, huh?" Lisa said.

"You're so much better at analogies than I
am. How'd that happen? You're right; it's a
funky place, huh?"

"I'll like it even more when we're inside and
drying off, quaffing cognac. Hey, look, he's
got a white 'vette. Nice."

"We might just have to turn around, you
know."

"He'd better let me use the bathroom, anyway."

They pulled into the lengthy driveway, got
out of the car, and made a dash for the front
door, sprinting across the flooded walk.

When they hit the stoop Lisa went up the porch steps while Katie ran the accompanying ramp she knew had been made for Jacob's wheelchair-bound brother. Under the veranda, out of the spray of the storm, they caught their breath.

"I just noticed something," Katie said.

"I wish you wouldn't. I hate when you notice things."

"There aren't any lights on."

"What were you expecting? A neon welcome sign?"

"Not even a porch light."

"He wasn't expecting company, and there's no one else around here to see it."

"It's not that late."

"Oh, stop." Heading for the front door, Lisa stumbled in the dark, took an awkward step, and banged her shin against one of the posts. She turned to see what had tripped her and stifled a cry when she saw that it was moving. "What is it?"

Katie stuck her foot out and prodded the smudge of blackness as it crept across the porch. "A turtle."

"Knock already."

"Me?"

"Yes, you, of course, you. Come on." Tonight they'd passed on into being goddamn ridiculous long ago, but did they really have to be assholes out on the porch? "Maybe you need to do this too much, Kathleen. You want to leave?" She desperately hoped it wouldn't be the case; she needed to go to the bathroom.

"No."

"Then knock."

# *Chapter Eleven*

He didn't dance with his sister.

Instead he followed her through the miasma of his nightmare. Shrugging off Elizabeth's grabbing hands, he pursued Rachel out through the closet door, into the folds of his room.

His body shivered on the bed, drenched with rain and sweat. Wind drove a harsher chill into his forehead and spine. If he lived, he might get pneumonia. His sister—with that bitter and knowing smile he considered as much a part of her as anything else, like a scar—turned to him and twirled again, gaping at the body in the bed, made kissy-kissy sounds, and licked his eyes.

*Sweet*, she said.

"Wow, you are fucked up."

*Look who judges.*

"Cut the crap; get to the point."

Beth watched from the closet doorway, unable to step outside. Hair tangled by their sex, her small breasts heaved, needing him all over again. The half circles under her eyes darkened, the flesh bunching like the scar tissue of someone beaten for years. He felt his family trying to slam the door shut in her face, everybody so petty with their histrionics, and he kept it open with an isolated force of will, pressing it back so hard that the plaster behind the doorknob broke away in chunks. The house squealed as if pinched.

*My*, his sister said. *Touchy, aren't we?*

"Yes, we are. We all are."

"Stay with me, Jacob," Beth pleaded, but all he could do was gesture for her to wait, wanting to tell her not to die but understanding even in the middle of the maelstrom how ridiculous that would sound—as if there were anywhere she might ever go, or that everything would be all right soon. He smiled wanly, but perhaps it meant something, that there were realizations being made. He had to see what Rachel might show him, and uncover the reasons why this was happening, to find out what had occurred ten years ago and when the hell it would end.

He let the door slowly close on her, as gently as he could. It was a way of keeping her safe in his room, secure in the place that remained a treasure of memory and whispers. Beth understood and waved sadly, tears rippling down her cheeks, catching in that clumped white tissue.

"Damn you for making me do this," he said to the dead.

*No, Third. Damn you for making me do this.*

There was no real feeling of movement as they crept upward to the roof—his body on the bed whimpering and fists snatching out in sleep, so unlike himself—where Jacob saw the sharp prongs of the weather vane displaying his brother's decapitated head, one eye crushed, the other awake and gaping; their mother's head was firmly stuck on the southern arrow, tongue lolling, lipstick smeared on her cheeks, her chin thick with rusty blood. Rachel patted him on the shoulder and took aim. He knew what she was doing before she grinned and threw herself forward, impaling her chest on another point, giggling and then grunting as the black metal ripped free through her back.

"Games," he said. "And not very impressive ones."

They looked at him, accusing but silent, slowly spinning in the storm. The weight of their stares became horribly imposing after a minute, threatening to grind him. He didn't mind mockery, so long as he could determine a purpose. Lightning reflected in their gazes, those eyes so full of curiosity and ridicule. Still so calm as the weather vane creaked, spikes dripping with viscera, a torrent of rain carrying the pink down across the tar near his feet.

*And those moonlit grins, why don't they scream? Why won't they talk? Mom's teeth gleaming, vocal chords unfurled and wagging in the wind, like her voice trying to slap at me. Joseph's upper lip curled in that arrogant sneer of superiority, slinging defamation.* His face fell in upon the same old lines, his scowl a tattoo. Rachel's torn heart hung from the tip of the arrow, turning and turning; she wasn't even wearing it upon her sleeve. Jacob took several steps forward, gripped the weather vane in both hands, and brought it to rest. If only he could do the same for them. Mom spoke but no sound came out. His eyes settled on nothing in particular as he asked, "Where is Dad?"

That's what it took.

Dad suddenly stood behind him, a firm but tender hand massaging the back of Jacob's neck, the way Mom used to do when he suffered through the infernal nights of migraines. Treetops bobbed around them. For a moment sunlight broke in, the past always battering at the present. He looked down and saw his mother in the garden, her face sweaty and her hands very tan, a heap of weeds piled beside her. Branches stirred. His father tried to tell him something in that touch, but Jacob kept wondering why the hell nobody would just come out and say it already.

He spun, desperately wanting to hug the man and express all he'd been trying to say these last ten years. "Dad, you've got to listen. . . ." But no, he didn't; none of them did, especially now as he looked into his father's ashen face tortured with wrinkles. There proved to be too much to be seen there, and yet also not enough; it was impossible to explain what it meant to live in the Maelstrom shadow, to be alive and yet follow the footsteps of the dead. Jacob stammered in meaningless moans, and Dad's soothing fingers dug a bit deeper into the knots of his son's neck. The crying *need* in the forest tried to scream into his ear again, but his father's protective hand held it away for a moment. Another kind of madness took precedence.

In his peripheral vision he spotted a haphazard motion flicking by. He turned and watched as Joseph's face began to quiver, muscle by muscle, rocking back and forth, building up momentum. Each nerve danced, tics high in his cheeks like a signature of arousal. With a final heave his brother's head fell from the pike, landed at Jacob's feet, and rolled, dragging its bleeding esophagus behind it. The puddles on the roof were deep enough that Joseph had to talk with half a mouthful of water. His voice came out warbling and gurgling, but distinctively happy. *For us, Third? You bring your company for us? Man, how I dig that redhead, the curves on her. Thank you.* His brother, full of sincerity. *Thank you.* It revolted him.

*Company?*

Jacob awoke thrashing in bed, his nostrils burning, his legs tangled up in his sheets. He sputtered metallic-tasting water, choking, maybe on the verge of drowning. Reaching over for the nightstand, he got a handhold to keep from falling onto the floor. Rain continued spattering inside, washing into his face. He'd been so close; some kind of answer had been within reach. His father had touched him.

*Redhead?*

"Oh, God." He got up to shut the window and could barely make out a car parked at the edge of the driveway. Who the hell could be there? What new players in the game? Reporters—had they found him again? Who else would the house swallow?

He ran from his room, and by the time he got to the stairway he heard the almost frenzied knocking.

# *Chapter Twelve*

He opened the door and stared out into the dark, swamped porch, catching only the slightest glint of moonlit reflection in two pairs of eyes—he still hadn't switched on the circuit breakers in the basement—and immediately saw the curves Joseph had mentioned. Which muse had been a redhead? Cardinal. And little red fox. An instant before a lightning flash showed off Lisa's beauty he realized it was her, that fiery hair almost glowing in the blackness.

In the flaring illumination he saw another woman standing to the right of the doorway, and knew the turtle had gazed upon her too but had no idea what that really meant, though clearly she was important. Had Wakely sent them to bring him out of Stonethrow, the man too scared to return by himself? How had Elizabeth reached him in his dreams?

The door had been open for four or five seconds already, his hand still jittery on the knob, and the women were getting drenched. What kind of an excuse could he give them to get them the hell out of here, now as he sensed the forest coming to life, those sounds out there rising under the cover of night, so much murmuring of love? *Jesus.*

He said, "This might sound a little crazy, but I think you . . ."

The ladies waited patiently, brushing their wet hair from their eyes, freezing on the veranda. Lisa opened her mouth to say something, to cut him off and explain what the hell they were doing, but all he could hear now was the abrupt shattering noise in the distance, a crash of falling tree and stone. His father had chosen the island to build on because it was so easy to snip the ties to the rest of civilization. Seclusion. Isolation. Jacob balled his hands into fists and dug them into his hips, knowing that the bridge to Stonethrow had just collapsed or been blocked.

"Hi, Jacob," Lisa said. "Listen, I know I've got some heavy explaining to do, but I hope we're not disturbing you. I've really got to use your bathroom. Would you mind if we came in?"

His brother dug redheads. *Oh, God.*

He smiled and tried to keep the tremolo out of his voice, but didn't do too good a job. "Not at all, Lisa. Glad to see you. Come inside before you catch pneumonia. Who's your friend?"

Lisa made the first move. She had to, seeing as how she wasn't even supposed to know where Jacob was, or care at all. She stepped inside as if it were the most natural situation in the world, hugging Jacob and rubbing his back in slow circles, only now realizing that this was actually fairly deep shit. He wouldn't call the cops or anything, would he? Who else was here? She introduced Katie and watched her best friend sort of slip out of herself for a second, that weird calm descending over her the way it sometimes did.

"Pleasure to meet you, Katie," Jacob said,

taking her hand. He pushed the front door shut, slapping out all light. His words echoed down the corridors. "The fuses must have blown. Just stand where you are and I'll be back in a minute."

"Okay," Lisa said.

"Just stand here; don't move."

"We will."

"All right."

They heard him rush off, his steps confident even in the total darkness, quick and knowing. "Is this the way you imagined it, Kathleen?"

"Yes, actually."

"You thinking this was a mistake?"

"Are you?"

"Well . . . he doesn't sound too happy to see us . . ." With her arms outstretched before her, Lisa felt around until she walked into a sheet-covered chair. "Too late now, though."

"Yes," Katie answered. "I think it has been for a while now."

Jacob had felt the unstrung tension in Katie's hand, a nervous quivering, like some of them had. He could tell when they knew too much about him, the way they gave a little bit extra, almost ready to hug him, just on the point of questioning him, and expecting the sluice gates to open wide. That handshake had been much more personal than Lisa's embrace. Who the hell was she?

He slammed the main circuit breaker and heard the buzzing flood of electricity as the house charged and came awake to its life. Someone had left the basement light on, and he saw his surroundings exactly as he remembered them. He walked over to the hot- and cold-water pipes, opened them, then hit the hot-water boiler, as if somebody might be here long enough to take a shower.

"What the hell are you planning?" he asked the deceased.

After a quick unveiling job, where he pulled geese-covered sheets off furniture and gave an inept dusting, the ladies sat on the couch in the living room while Jacob scouted the kitchen cabinets for whatever might have been left behind. With the lights on he had to fight the traction of the past again; whatever he saw dragged him backward. Here, this scrape of wood on the wall, he'd done that when he was six, having accidentally fallen in his chair while leaning over reaching for a comic book. And these marks on the floor, Rachel's tap shoes; it was inconceivable that no one had managed to wax them away. This broken handle on the oven from where Mom burned the Thanksgiving bird and Dad, afraid of fire, had yanked the oven door open too hard and ripped the handle right off, holding it like Charlie Chaplin, just looking at it, then trying to jam it back into place; more, so much more, everywhere his gaze set down. This flux and flow of the familiar. He cursed his perfect memory.

He found tea and made a pot. The back of his neck crept as he glanced at the piano.

Lisa said, "It was stupid of us not to have packed anything. Sorry we're forcing you to play host. I know you weren't expecting anyone."

"No, I wasn't."

Her eyebrows fluttered a little, as though she was trying to lighten the mood. "Um, yeah, well . . ."

Jacob sat on the piano stool, as if wanting to spite his brother, almost daring him to reclaim the chair, wondering if he should play a piece as sort of a dare, maybe something with the taste of a fugue.

Katie and Lisa sipped their tea. He sat and watched them, and it went on like that for a long while, until he finally asked, "Did Bob tell you where I'd be?"

"No," Lisa said.

"I see."

Katie said, "Mr. Maelstrom, it's actually my fault." He grimaced, the stupid alliteration of his name catching him wrong again. She noticed and cocked her head. "Lisa was just doing me a favor. You see, I'm writing my thesis . . . dissertation, actually, and she knew how much it meant to me to—"

"Katie," Lisa said. She knew her friend when she got like this, all the words about to rush out in one long, ridiculous stream that would make them both look even more foolish than they already felt. In Bob's office, Jacob had seemed witty, amiable, and good-natured, everything that he didn't appear to be now. They'd fouled something up horribly, and she only hoped they could backtrack out of here without doing too much damage.

"Look, I'm not letting you get into trouble for—"

"It's all right," he told them, like a teacher breaking up a squabble at the playground.

Lisa actually blushed. She couldn't remember the last time she'd blushed; it didn't happen like this often because she never put herself in these situations. She knew better than to spill it out. Now, how to explain she'd sneaked into Bob's desk and gotten the directions and spent hours traveling in circles on muddy roads all so Katie could question Jacob at length about ... what? Were they going on a treasure hunt, find a map somewhere, get a dripping candle to carry, slide along the wall until they came upon the secret spinning bookcase, go down a flight of creaking stairs and dig in the basement until they found somebody's head?

"So you're writing your dissertation on my father," Jacob said.

Katie grinned without humor, staring closely at him now, his perceptive goodwill frown. She must've gotten it a lot to know it so well, to do it without even realization. He wondered what kind of doctors had stared at her, and why? "Actually, Jacob, it's more of an analytical comparison between the arc of your career so far and the body of your father's works."

Now, didn't that sound nice. "I don't talk about my father," he said.

"Yes, I know."

A button pusher, but not with a sneer. Katie had a near-confrontational disposition, but the kind that would never actually get her into a fight. An offbeat mixture of curiosity and conflict. Jacob told her, "Since I was eighteen there have been five nonfiction books published detailing my works inclusively or in connection with my father's. Three of them were written by Robert Wakely."

"Those were essays that dealt with the works from an utterly impersonal point of view, hoping to cash in more on the events of your past than on your writing itself. There is much more to discern in your allusions, plots, convolutions, and the subject matter of your novels. Especially when one takes into consideration your age. They're all wrong, those essayists. They all missed the mark."

Yes, they had. The mark, the bloody mark, all these stains. But he had to ask anyway: "What mark might that be?"

Katie couldn't help herself; hard as she tried she couldn't stop now that she'd started. *Fadeaway, Crossing Christ, Sweat on the Window, Surgery of the Claw, Sins of the Sons,* each new title taking up a specific place in a linear saga, those words always the same, like her grandfather's leather had always been the same, vocabulary and underlining theme utilized over and over to greater advantage.

She pulled a microcassette tape recorder out of her purse and turned it on without asking his permission. She could imagine him reaching over in one liquid movement and smashing it with his fist, taking her by the throat, hissing in her face, but he did nothing. She stared him in the eye; it felt good to be looking there, as if finally meeting the painter of the Rorschach test, so that you could ask him just what the hell he'd meant when he did it. What did he see? Because that would really be the right answer.

Nobody realized the rain had stopped, though the clouds continued to roil. Katie told him everything she thought about all of his stories, and how she compared them to his father's, and to his own past. Every once in a while Lisa groaned, from chagrin or boredom. Jacob said nothing. On occasion he looked at the portrait of Taddy, as if for guidance. Katie sat with the teacup squeezed in her hand, nearly panting after talking for so long, unsure of exactly what she'd said. She gazed at him, leaning forward in his direction, on the end of the couch, waiting for him to say something. Waiting. Waiting.

Waiting.

Jacob stood and went to the door, looked out at the porch. He glanced down at the turtle, feeling the momentum of revelations hurtling toward him.

A flash of memory stole to the surface: Rachel lying by the river, legs spread wide with fingers caressing the meat of her inner thighs, shorts and bikini underwear pulled down to her ankles. A possum bending its head, gazing at him, washing itself with rapidly skittish hands rubbing over its face, and Jacob feeling his sister's heat. He spit on the animal in the midst of a blurring white light, as Rachel bucked her hips toward him. A man with rough features hunched over her and began to grunt. Groans rose from the brush where Jacob had run to hide.

# *Chapter Thirteen*

*Okay, so sometimes it's got to be like this.*

*You do your own thing, you don't think it all the way through, and you pay for it later because it's got to be paid for.*

"I don't believe it," Lisa said, fluffing smelly pillows behind her neck. "How does this kind of shit always happen to me? Amazing. I feel as if we've been sent to bed. Punished."

"I think we have been," Katie said from the other bed across the room. She sat up and with a firm chop of her hand, an ax blade in its own right, sliced down, trying to cut off the conversation. "I don't want to talk about it any more. Let's just get some sleep."

"Easy for you to say."

"Yeah, right, easy for me to say."

"I mean, you're taking it in stride."

"No, I'm not."

"You seem to be."

"So what the hell does that mean?"

"Nothing."

"Look, you're sleeping with your boss; how much jeopardy can your job be in? Can we get some sleep?"

"Oh, that's nice, Kathleen, that's very nice."

"I'm sorry."

"Who's going to be able to sleep in this place? You? I was more comfortable twisted up in the backseat. How do they know he didn't do it? Found a way to lock himself in the closet; shit, how hard can that be?"

Jacob hadn't said anything after Katie's discourse, and she'd gotten the feeling she could have waited all night long and he still wouldn't have said anything. What else could she expect? She wondered if he was simply more jaded by the attention than anything else. She'd seen the look on his face, the hinges of his jaw pulsing, and could tell that the anguish of being the only survivor bore down on him, as if his family's murderer still chased him around the house.

"Did you see his eyes?" she asked.

"Told you he was cute."

"No, not that."

*Those eyes.*

She'd stared into them for entranced minutes, trying to pry loose the boards that covered the broken windows of his soul. How stupid; after everything, she couldn't recall their color now. He hadn't said anything afterward; he merely stood and motioned for them to follow him upstairs. They followed him through a confusing trail of winding stairwells and twisted corridors, ramps, and doorways. Jacob had found some plastic-covered pillows and blankets carefully put away in the linen closet. After searching out the cleanest room, he had led the ladies down another hall to a bedroom where they could spend the night.

The smells, though. *Jesus.*

The bulb in the lamp on the nightstand had long since burned out, and he replaced it with one he found working in the room next door. Katie had tried to grab hold of his attention, in a halfhearted attempt to apologize in case there was something to be sorry for—there was always something to be sorry for—but there was no chance of talking to his back like that.

When at last he spoke it had been with a hollow smile that sent pins veering in her belly. "My bedroom is there, in the northwest corner"—he pointed to what was presumably the northwest—"a couple doors over from the landing, down the corridor, on the left side. The house is an acoustic auditorium. If you need anything you can just shout and I'll hear you, but I'm afraid I don't have much to offer." Oh, yes, he definitely meant that the way he said it, with the emphasis smacking down hard on the final words. She wondered if he could have done it. For whatever reason an eleven-year-old kid flips out and massacres his family, and then has the guts and the gall to lock himself in the closet for days, until he nearly dies of starvation and thirst himself. *He has nothing to give.* "Hope you'll overlook the state of the room, but it does have its own toilet." He opened the door and flicked on the light, checked to see if there was paper. There was, though both Lisa and Katie stared at each other thinking how gritty it looked; they'd never touch themselves with that. "And there's a tub and shower stall if you need one now or in the morning. Let the water run awhile; there's bound to be a lot of rust in the pipes. Sleep well. Good night."

And that had proven to be that.

"Yes," Lisa said. "I saw his eyes."

# Chapter Fourteen

Lumber had been smashed, the rapids battering the scraps of wood ceaselessly into the rocks. The bulk making up the underside braces were mostly splinters now, railings having fallen through into the other beams. Most of the bridge resided underwater in the churning whitecaps, the rest downriver, heading into the lake. The remaining frame had scorch marks—lightning had struck the opposite end, and a fire had raged across its entire length.

More games, but at least with some style this time.

He drove back to the house, not wanting to be away any longer than necessary, passing the pond and feeling the *need* drawing him in.

He rolled down the window, as if any of them could hear him. "Tough. I need, too. Everyone does. You're not so damn special." Jacob pressed the heel of his hand against his forehead, smelling the gardens of his mother, so much dirt everywhere. The pain intensified, and his vision doubled. Nausea corkscrewed through him, and bile rose. He stopped the car and staggered out, gasping, and rested against the hood of the 'vette. In a moment the woods came to life, bushes parting to reveal lithe forms and arching backs, angry faces in the brush.

His many muses. His children.

Someone cried, like calling after the ice-cream man down the block, "Liege, Liege . . ."

He turned and spotted a few more, arms waving, then all of them coming for him, crawling in the mud the way they always did. He limped off toward the pond, knowing there was safety to be found there, but not certain why. Fatigue and resignation cut further into his head as they scrambled toward him. Hands caught his ankles. He hit the ground, scrambling on all fours, too tired to move and yet moving anyway. He grabbed fistfuls of wild grass and pulled himself along in the dirt. The left side of his rib cage felt cracked, something missing there. Another handful of grass and another few inches, he felt himself heading toward an answer. The need wanted him.

Lucifer.

And Salome came dancing in his green dreams.

Water splashed as bodies tumbled around him, nails and claws lightly brushing his back. Someone straddled his back and then went rolling off. Padding footsteps came easing up the shore. Moonlight shimmered, skimming the surface of the pond. Lips moved to his, other breaths abruptly beating in his chest, filling his lungs. It became a strangely sexual odyssey as a tongue pressed deeply past his lips, mouth crushing against his own. The kiss went on, touching the fillings of his back teeth, licking inside his cheek as if trying to draw the pond out of him.

He thought it might be Beth, or perhaps

even Katie; but no, this other lover was neither of them. He knew this kind of a caress, though, brushing the mud from his face and hair, clearing his ears. Insects buzzed madly, and he felt a faintly stirring wind brushing them away. The rain began again and played across the water once more, those fingers moving and probing his body.

*I know these hands.*

Of course he did.

Jacob mouthed her name and opened his eyes, searching. He tried pulling himself up but couldn't quite make it, and floundered back to hit the ground once more. Death held its own charms. He tightened his stomach muscles and tried again, hefting himself forward.

You live, he thought; you're alive. "I'm alive?"

He was dead.

She knelt beside him at the edge of the pond, her feet in the water, drenched as she should always be. Draped in silt and mire, her emerald and blond hair flowed with the drizzle washing down her pallid face. The night surrounding her blossomed to life. Someone tittered; another sobbed. Her eyes were still full of gold, and slit like a lizard's, huge and bashful, even as she stuck her hand under his shirt. Her teeth moved in toward his neck, nipping.

When she blinked you could almost hear the sound of it in the air—*ba-leenk, ba-leenk,* eyelashes swiping and tickling him as she nuzzled closer. Those powerful legs drew against him, strong enough to send him up from the depths of murder in the pond. Large breasts, the way his brother had ordered them in his fantasies, always the same, so big and round, but topped with smallish, pink nipples. Face as beautiful as their lust had made it. Here she remained, beside him even now: the water nymph, his oldest daughter, his first lover in blood.

Ophelia.

"I've been waiting, Liege," she told him.

In the rain, with the glow of the bulging moon overhead, a spear of sunlight suddenly stabbed down, another section of the past unfolding. He turned his head and saw his brother on the shore beside him, only pretending to be asleep, his rage so alive that it peered out beneath his tan skin. He watched himself as a child digging his feet in the sand. Rachel tugged a lock of Jacob's wet hair and curled it around her finger. That was the beginning, just before they began what would destroy them. Then the gushing darkness poured into the gap with a wave of black ink, filling the shaft of sunlight from the bottom up until only the night remained. Ophelia's breath caught as she dropped forward and began sobbing against his chest.

Jacob hugged her. "I know."

Leaning over, he took her even more tightly into his arms, her skin slippery with the pond scum, coating her as if she were newborn. This misfortune of not being able to touch anyone had become a hideous motif. He looked beyond her shoulder and saw the indistinct outlines of other men and women standing in the forest, lying upon the logs, sweltering in the storm. The rest of his muses, loyal and willing lovers abounding, whispered and cooed at him as they approached.

His father had written a bad line once: *Our Edens must be corrupted if we are to become the only gods.*

He couldn't help smiling, as she *ba-linked* at him once more. He understood that at last he'd be joining the rest of his family, and only wished he could tell them now that he'd never been the lucky one, being left alive. He hoped they wouldn't continue to resent him from the other side of hell. "I'm a ghost." Ophelia's webbed hand smoothed back his hair. He didn't think he was breathing much anymore.

His pulse tapped out an incredibly slow rhythm. Looking down at his hands, rubbing them together, he couldn't tell the difference between his own life and death anymore.

"You are legion because you have the most to offer." A loud array of growls and laughter seemed to second her beliefs. "We're your family; we are here for you. We have always been here for you."

Of course they were. Jacob got to his feet and dropped over again, puzzled as to why he was so weak after murder and the other dead were so powerful. Muses came to him and kneeled, pranced, and shimmied in the grass. He said, "What did Rachel do with their heads?"

Ophelia's lengthy tresses twisted in the breeze and blew across her face, and she plucked the strands and reset them behind her ears. In a voice filled with devotion and piety, much more than anyone should ever be doomed to have, she said, "You must rest, Lucifer; you're close to death."

He curled in the mud like a snake and hissed; "Don't ever call me that."

His muses backed off. Ophelia shrank from him until she was chest-deep in the water. Her bottom lip quivered, large golden eyes growing still wider as rivulets of pond water and rain ran down the incline of her nose, and over the soft scales of her chin. "But—"

"It's not my name."

"It is."

"No, it's a lie told to you by my brother and sister." Being one of the deceased calmed him, even as his wrath took on a more substantial shape. "And I will destroy them for it."

Weeping, Ophelia's crying excited the others in the darkness. He heard them all whimpering among themselves, afraid to face this light of the light-bearer, Lucifer. She covered her face with her thin, ashen fingers, refusing even to look at him any longer. The trees rustled with climbing bodies jumping through the branches. Musk filled his lungs, finally overpowering the fragrance of his mother's lilies. Wood snapped all around them. And then only a swelling silence from the many throats: Sparrow, Deer, Possum, Thrush, Cardinal, little red Fox, whom Joseph had taught to laugh, even that raccoon who'd moved upon his sister's haunches.

He slipped further and further into the water and waded through the pond until he stood with her again. How selfish a father he had proven to be, even worse than his own. He lifted Ophelia's chin and took her hand, leading her back to the shore. He held her once more, and hid his face against her slick neck, kissing her passionately. She responded with a gasp.

"I've failed you and the others," he said, unsure of his own meaning. Muses clapped and wailed, and there was splashing. "I'm too weak." He reached down to feel his missing rib, unsure of what he was any longer, or what he'd ever been. "I don't know why my family died, why I've got to be dead."

Now, with his hand stuffed into his mouth, he bit deeply and tasted his own blood, knowing it was poison but that there was arcana in it, all kinds of different Edens and hells and alchemy.

She worked his fist free and brought his wound to her lips. "Do you recall our love-making?" she asked.

The moon ignited her yellow stare.

"Yes," he said, and the others moaned all around him. That was the beginning, just before they began what would destroy them. "I remember."

# *Chapter Fifteen*

This was how it got sometimes, on the bad nights when the panic attacks hit, and the dust in the high corners and all over the place fell away to ashes and anxiety. Maybe it was just her minor case of asthma acting up, but it felt like all her high school years pressing in, each awkward lover in her face, mauling her breasts like a baby nipping and sucking, the way she didn't want it to be, though on occasion she thought she might.

"Damn."

Lisa sneezed again; the dust in the musty room was crucifying her allergies, but Katie had forbidden her to open the window any more than two inches for fear of chills in the night. Katie could be like that: one minute as unconstrained as possible, the next playing the role of grandmother with an obsessive-compulsive tack. It seemed to be something left over from the hospital, keeping the windows closed all the time, like they had guards in gun turrets; you open the window and they slap the spotlight on you and start shooting.

Chills, now that was almost funny. What else were you supposed to get in a place like this, under these circumstances, where *decapitations*, for Christ's sake, had occurred. She kept thinking about it, wishing she'd actually read Bobby's books now, so she could have prepared a little. How she didn't know, but the vision of heads rolling around like bowling bowls wouldn't let up. A giant spider spinning a web, you're trying to get away and run right into it, you're stuck and screaming, and turn to your left and what's there but a couple of skulls with the eyes still perfect but hanging all the way out. You look right and there's a couple more. You pull your arms but the gummy strands have got you, and when you finally look up there's the spider with its hairy legs bearing down. In this house you could believe every bad horror movie you'd ever seen, especially with a cute guy with an innocent front and a hidden attitude meandering about. Yes, you got the chills.

And also there was the smell.

She spun over again, punched the feather-filled pillow once more, raising more dust so that she had to shield her face. She sneezed five or six times, rapid-fire. Yanking the sheet over her shoulder she tried to get more comfortable, wondering what it all meant, if any of this was actually going to help Katie in the long run, or just make her worse. She dwelled on Bob for a while and then drove the thoughts out, because with him came the face of the baby.

That image wavered for a second, like rippling water, the infant like a beautiful lizard, covered in her blood; then she saw it with a toothless smile, looking like Bobby, the same angle of the nose, prominent forehead, yet with wisps of her red hair. Each ripple took her a bit farther on. The kid with some teeth, two tiny ones, drool leaking, hands up reaching and yanking, and Lisa seeing herself from the back walking toward the baby, standing behind herself and witnessing the moment.

She couldn't tell what might register on her own face, if she was smiling or grimacing, whether she reached for the kid to hold and hug, or merely to shake it. Lisa kept hoping to move farther into the image, to cruise around inside it a little, drift over to the left, so she could see what registered there in her own face, and get an idea of how it might be. But whenever she moved, the other Lisa moved, too, blocking her off so that she could see the child but never herself.

The kid was grinning, but they always grinned; it meant nothing. She wanted to tap herself on the shoulder, get her to turn around, talk with herself for a while, and see exactly how bad or good it was. But even though her hand sometimes made it into the image, so that she could see herself reaching for that other Lisa's shoulder, she wouldn't turn around to talk. It seemed like the other Lisa knew she was being followed by herself, and she either despised this Lisa or just didn't give a shit anymore.

Listening to Katie's soft snores did nothing to improve her frame of mind. How much longer would it take to gather whatever material she needed for her paper or her dreams, whatever she needed? Tomorrow morning,

Jesus, let them get out of here as soon as possible.

Lisa sat up in bed and shot off another series of dry sneezes. The tenth or eleventh one started to hurt, the center of her chest tight and painful. Rain spattered down across the window. She held her hand over her face like an oxygen mask, trying to keep the dust out, to hold the air down in her lungs. Finally she could breathe again, and flopped back on the mattress. "Damn."

So she had the kid on her mind, after all. Along with it came Robert, too, the doctor's address, and, really, when it came down to it, no guilt, except when she thought of Katie and Timothy, and how the loss had affected them. All their voices ran together in her mind like a symphony, Tim's especially, both sides of him—the sweet guy with a grin that made her flush, and the coke-freak maniac who had pounded Katie into a quivering, terrified animal. High, lilting notes, low staccato, an argument without words, just a few throaty growls and hums that she added to the song as she fought off another sneeze, feeling the drag of musty air in her throat.

And she heard music.

It took her a moment to realize it wasn't in her mind but in the house: such a deliberate and laggard tune, with a couple of seconds' pause between notes on the piano, as though the player were hesitant in the playing of his song or unsure of where each key lay, distracted or afraid of touching the ivory. But soon the notes flowed faster, the pianist gaining confidence quickly as the composition grew steadily into something with charm. The chords came together much more smoothly, that melody a somber but classical piece, played out with a sort of bop, jazzy twist. She wasn't sure if she liked it or not.

And now, Jacob quietly singing.

She swung out of bed and got dressed, feeling the exhaustion hit her full tilt when she stood. Her back and shoulders ached, and she moved about as slowly as a geriatric, doing some stretches in the hopes of loosening up some. Her neck crackled in a way it never had before and she went, "Uhy." She sat back on the mattress and put on her shoes, the dust pressing her out. She left the room and stepped into the wide hall.

Snarls of corridors and vestibules bounced the distant sounds back to her from odd angles, echoes up in the corners spiking down at her. Lisa spun, and spun again, the music reaching out from behind her now, as if from the walls. Why hadn't she paid more attention?

There were stairwells all over, short, squat steps that looked hammered together in the garage, a much grander stairway at the end of the passage. Oil paintings depicted common scenes of children playing in the fields and fishermen pulling in their nets. Empty brass candlestick holders sat atop thin mantles that ran half the length of the hallway, the wood cracked in places, as though one of these writers hadn't been able to finish a chapter and had come out here to thump his head. Small glass lights shaped like flowers jutted from both sides of the corridor every five or six feet; others were ersatz oil-burning lamps that looked minutes from fracturing with age. Very few had been turned on, allowing only a thin and irksome illumination.

Each door she passed appeared to be of heavy oak, the kind you could fling yourself against and pound on as jungle cats stalked calmly behind you, nobody on the other side ever hearing you hammering until your hands were broken and a pool of blood seeped underneath.

"Jesus," she said. "What the hell am I thinking about?"

The Maelstroms had harbored a keen fetish

for a security and antiquity. Cushioned chairs sat outside many of the rooms, as well as umbrella stands, those high-standing ashtrays filled with sand that she didn't think you'd find anywhere outside of a hotel, and lots of coatracks. She wondered if they'd thrown many parties before all the reclusiveness and panic. Bob had never told her anything about this place, whether he'd had a lot of fun here before the gore.

Lisa looked back down the hall and couldn't decide which bedroom she'd left Katie in, or how long she'd been walking. The floor seemed to tilt a bit, throwing off her line of sight, relations changing from step to step. What would that do for your perspective, to never feel anything too familiar from one inch to the next? She entered a vestibule, another hall, much shorter, but with a serpentine twisting, the walls curved here, and extremely shiny, as if waxed smooth. She admired the woodwork, and could respect the effort that had gone into this ugly, demented house. She cut left and found herself in an alcove that ended with a large, unattractive door. Some of this stuff should have been in a palace; the rest appeared to have fallen off a truck. She backed up, imagining what they must have written about here, how many times monsters had roamed down this same dead-end, a heroine about as stupid as she was standing here with a candle and trying the knob.

So where the hell was she in this goddamn labyrinth? Rooms distended, the hall widening and narrowing, and she was surprised to find that lights randomly checkered the house. Jacob must've snapped on every switch in the mansion, but about three-quarters of the bulbs were burned out. "Shit, you've got to be kidding me. I could've been at the beach," she muttered, feeling exceedingly tired, and just wanting to get back to bed now. Maybe they would keep the kid.

It was cold, and she rubbed her forearms, the gooseflesh bringing on even more chills. She moved along without any noise of creaking floorboards, the hall with a sloping bend to it, like an intestine using peristalsis to shove her through. "Oh, that's good; that's a nice, nice analogy." Even the paintings varied only slightly in content and style, no portraits with memorable glares or smiles.

She tilted her head, listening, and could still hear the music. The singing sounded no closer or farther than before. She found it hard to keep from stumbling, walking as if on an inclined plane.

Of course, it made sense; some of the floors were ramps. There was no elevator, though, so the poor guy in the wheelchair had just . . . what, rolled around? She started to rush, flung open a couple of doors, though she didn't expect any escape there, just for the hell of it now, to see what could be seen. Incredibly, there was no way out, and she wasn't sure if she'd just been going in circles. Because of the curve she couldn't see the end of the corridor no matter which way she checked. It made her giggle, and that scared her. Rotted molding crackled; water must be leaking through the walls. She sneezed again and started coughing, feeling blood trickling in the back of her throat. She couldn't quite catch her breath.

Where was that other stairway now? *Fuck it.* She had to get back to Katie, and back to Bob. *An acoustic auditorium? What bullshit.* A museum was more like it, a Jersey pier carnival haunted house complete with phantom creaks, echoes, and a soundtrack with a jazzy beat. A place where murderers smiled at you, and lived in the same house.

*What if his sister didn't do it?*

*What if he did?*

A kid of eleven, swinging an ax, killing his whole family?

"No, impossible. It's got to be impossible." Couldn't you outrun an eleven-year-old heaving an ax?

A house where grinning killers made flashing snatches for your ankles; she could feel those shadows like angry vise-grip presences whenever they played across her. Okay, so it was getting a little weird, and that smell, it kept after her. She was definitely walking uphill now, and she waited for the lights to turn red and go strobe, the funhouse to really start in with the action. She looked in the high corners for the giant spider with the corpses in its web. She covered her nose and mouth, the air so heavy and musty here. She raised her arms up higher in a protective manner, like a linebacker going in for a block, maybe to guard herself if she should walk full tilt into a mirror that would shatter and gut her. *Oooh, fun, fun, fun, there's always fun in the house of horror.*

Yes, you got the chills.

Tears heated her cheeks and she realized she was starting to let go. She murmured names but didn't even know whose they were. How could she call for Jacob now while thinking of him, a little boy with those eyes, grinning and a trail of somebody else's blood splashed across his forehead? Maybe Bob found the crazy kid in the closet and cleaned him up, didn't want to send an eleven-year-old off to an institution for the rest of his life, took pity on Jacob.

The beach sounded so good that she stopped reaching for the other Lisa and started trying to shove her with both hands, imploring her to run, to go get Bob, to get him to come back here and help this Lisa somehow. Could Katie come down here and save her? She started walking faster, and even a little faster, not quite running; she wouldn't do that, no.

*Well, maybe.* She realized there was somebody behind her now. Maybe only the turtle again, or the soul of the child alive inside her waiting to fill its own skin. Or the beckoning dead, or yet *another* Lisa trying to turn *her* around, arm outstretched, hoping to get Lisa to look her in the eyes, to see if this life were the right one to take.

Her breath came in ragged gasps, and now she sort of limped along, getting away from Lisa, for whom she had no advice. Christ, didn't she know this was all fucked up? What would she ask, and what would she answer? Insanity, that anyone could keep up with anyone being chased around these halls. Her lungs were on fire now, sweat slipping down her back, urging her on through the belly of the house.

"Kathleen?" she whispered. "Jacob?"

A wheelchair rolled in front of her.

From the deepest heart of malice came a sick laughter.

# Chapter Sixteen

He remembered.

Sunlight. Fiery in the early morning, and flaring with needles of awe-inspiring rose and gold. A brilliance that lavishes the world with freckles of a burning aura that makes him squint and leaves him blind whenever he shambles into the dark house for potato chips and cherry Kool-Aid.

Staring up at those tremendous clouds bearing down, as soft and appealing as his sister's kisses, he knows the world is about to shift. The acute blue of the sky is as lovely as it should be; the bushy canopy branches of the great trees looming a hundred feet high above continue to cross-thatch as if reaching with loving arms, but his skin crawls. Surrounding him on all sides are the giant trunks grounded forever in the rocky earth. Everywhere leaves waft in the wind, jetting from the woods, kicked up by the currents, trailing as if in a jet stream, and rolling lazily in the air. It's hot in the middle of August, a perfect day to play.

They're in a line, these three, positioned in the manner they've found themselves falling into, which is how it's meant to be: first, second, third. Joseph, Rachel, Jacob, lying on a large beach towel. Thirty toes dappling the pond, twenty of them occasionally moving, flicking at the minnows.

The water is clear, so clean that even when you kicked up the mud on the bottom it would just linger for a moment and settle back, as if drawn down. Eighty feet deep in the center, so Dad had told them; the pond would breathe them in. Jacob went swimming with his sister, flailing and splashing around its majestic pentacle-shaped breadth. Rachel would heave herself over him, both of them touching bottom, whirling around each other like streamers.

They would skinny-dip most mornings through their secrets. Sometimes the seclusion would hurt, but usually it didn't. There had been a couple of bad scares in the city, a failed kidnapping plot, and one lunatic who'd dragged Rachel into a car that had stalled a couple of blocks away, where she'd made a run for it, her nose broken. The island offered a little more safety: empty of townsfolk intruders and all of their father's more brazen fans, the ones that walked up with suspicious square packages wrapped in butcher paper, maybe only first-edition books they wanted signed or perhaps something more. The ones that always made everybody want to call the bomb squad first thing.

Mom and Dad would probably have fits if they knew—rushing for their library textbooks dealing with incest. Three kids lying here naked, not so young anymore, really. Rachel so beautiful that no one could possibly resist her, especially a boy on the verge of puberty whose breathing could hitch just by staring at the jut of her jaw, and an eighteen-year-old paraplegic with arms that could snap a spine in a moment of passion, in an instant of endless rage.

But Mother prefers to spend her days in the gardens and the orchards behind the house, and Dad never comes to the pond before dusk, when the atmosphere turns into something he can use in his warlock hunter McNellis of Ariovagne pieces. Or for his *Strange Water Tales*: he has a series of them, fourteen so far, all dealing with the ocean. Taddy Malstromo had even made a few cameo appearances as a demonic captain haunting the Sargasso, hunting for alien vessels in the sentient seaweed. Dad stays in his study writing, reading, researching, and re-typing drafts until sunset.

Joseph.

Joseph writhes.

Welding his eyes shut, he still witnesses his sister becoming a woman with all of the original sins they carry. She is *woman* to him. What else could be expected—school dances? Roller skating, first kisses, and corsages? Prom night, futzing with bra straps, backseat groping, the singles bars and singles ads? If only he'd gone away, anywhere, college, his own apartment, but the pull of the maelstrom is always too strong, and had dragged him back in now matter how hard he fought. At the age of eighteen he's had only one sexual encounter—two years ago in Manhattan

Join the Leisure Horror Book Club and
## GET 2 FREE BOOKS NOW—
## An $11.98 value!

### — Yes! I want to subscribe to — the Leisure Horror Book Club.

Please send me my **2 FREE BOOKS**. I have enclosed $2.00 for shipping/handling. Each month I'll receive the two newest Leisure Horror selections to preview for 10 days. If I decide to keep them, I will pay the Special Members Only discounted price of just $4.25 each, a total of $8.50, plus $2.00 shipping/handling. This is a **SAVINGS OF AT LEAST $3.48** off the bookstore price. There is no minimum number of books I must buy and I may cancel the program at any time. In any case, the **2 FREE BOOKS** are mine to keep.

*— Not available in Canada. —*

NAME: _____

ADDRESS: _____

CITY: _____ STATE: _____

COUNTRY: _____ ZIP: _____

TELEPHONE: _____

E-MAIL: _____

SIGNATURE: _____

If under 18, Parent or Guardian must sign. Terms, prices, and conditions subject to change. Subscription subject to acceptance. Dorchester Publishing reserves the right to reject any order or cancel any subscription.

while Dad had been doing a signing tour, and that night had been completely ludicrous, a reckless failure as much as a sloppy success. He'd made it with a friendly prostitute who'd had seductive wrinkles at the corners of her mouth, the softest lips imaginable, except when he imagines his sister. A middle-aged woman with a perfect hourglass shape, who'd agreed to accept him only so long as they screwed in his wheelchair. She was going to have some fun, go for the kink, yeah, do it in the wheelchair with the brake off. She'd taken him out of the only thing worse than pity— curiosity. To see the mighty man with muscles like plates of steel above dwindle into the matchstick freak, the nerves in the head of his cock raging, but his balls dead. Her grin had been so wide and hideous he'd had to hold his face against her breast to keep the bile down.

Comfort came in protective arrogance and wrath, as it did for all of them caught in the maelstrom. He chews his tongue, satisfied for the moment, almost glad that his father had taken to this hiding away. Though Rachel has seen his twisted legs for most of her life, he fears her seeing their skeletal shape now, and so pushes himself farther into the pond water until he's covered to the muscular notches of his abdomen.

Jacob sees it, and knowing his brother, and his sister, as well as knowing himself, he understands why. He's often dreamed that he'd grow into a great writer like his father, marry a woman with the same smile as his mother, and travel the cities of the world, eventually coming back to Stonethrow with his wife and children, setting up in this same house. He hoped that Rachel and Joseph wanted these same things, and could see all the children playing like in a playground, though there's no possibility it will become the truth.

He and Rachel swim for a time and then nap on the blanket in the tall grasses, drying out beside their brother, in correct sequence. They are on their backs looking into the branches, at the birds, and Jacob started admiring the brilliant colors of the fish. As if a pipe appeared from nowhere to repeatedly come down hard on his thoughts, they shattered, like the stained-glass window. The barbs of his conscience yank hard inside his chest, and he says, "I'm sorry, Rache."

She props herself up on an elbow, the smooth curve of her breast now angling outward, the nipple hard and pointed, as if accusing him. "Will you quit saying that, creepo? That's about the millionth time. There's nothing to apologize for, so forget it. Give it a break already."

He sits and draws closer to her, his penis semierect, as it usually is when lying this near, so nothing is apparently unnatural or abnormal. He searches for the correct words, his voice ineffectual and pleading. "I could have hurt you; I didn't mean to do it. I don't know. I got wrapped up in the game. It gets crazy, you know it, you like to piss me off so much . . . but . . . even so, still . . ." Warlock hunter McNellis of Ariovagne would never have thrown his sword at a lady; he would have held her first, his slouch hat covering his eyes, and made his apologies before he'd drawn his blade.

Jacob needs for her to believe him when he says he meant no malice, though he's uncertain if he's convinced himself. She hasn't told him yet she understands any of this, simply waving it away like shooing a fly, the meat of her breast quivering each time she did it, so that he liked it at first.

"Rache—"

"Shut up."

"But, listen, if you—"

"Shut up, Third."

Again the name, like a poker in the kidney,

putting him in last place, as always, forever. He leans back and rests his head on his hands. He wants to say that he wishes it could be like this forever, but there is no value in that, no purpose to the grimaces it would incite. So he shuts up.

A thousand leaves chase each other overhead, looping, circling, breezing by until caught in her hair. Her eyebrows are thick with pollen, like soot drifting into her gaze. His chest feels tight but he's not sure why. He realizes how unhappy they are, his brother and sister; everyone stewing, it comes off them like heat. All the anxiety and resentment—toward their parents, this place, where life took on a different form and meaning. It seems like she wants everything except what she already has. And where does that leave him, if she should leave him, wheeling Joseph away?

Eyes shut, Joseph only pretends to sleep, his rage so alive in him that it peers out beneath his skin. The veins in his arms and chest and neck and penis pulse with hatred. The rhythm of his breathing is a ragged beat, listening to every gesture made as Rachel tugs a lock of Jacob's wet hair and curls it around her finger. "If you want to know what

I really wish for in my heart of hearts, I'll tell you."

"Yes, tell me."

"Are you sure?"

"Yes, I'm sure."

"I'll tell you if you're positive."

"Yes, please."

She notices goose bumps on her pink aureole and dries the remaining drops off her chest with a corner of the towel. Jacob watches, fascinated by the texture of her breasts, how they stir and move and change depending on temperature, position. She has let him touch them, on occasion, though never long enough to satisfy his curiosity or arousal. It wouldn't be possible.

She says, "To leave."

That's not an answer, and he realizes she is only working up to the reality of one. "You want to leave?"

"Yes."

His bottom lip curls in trepidation. Out of all of them, she's the only one who might actually move on. "Where would you go?"

"Anywhere, of course. Who really cares? Anyplace. We're wealthy, we're famous, we ought to be in Manhattan, the East Village, Los Angeles at least, doing the clubs, playing the scene like a fife."

"A fife?"

"Wandering through the movie sets of those shitty films they make out of Dad's books. He should take them up on doing cameos; we could do walk-ons. If only he did more interviews—hell, they ask him all the time. He'd rather be here, up in the attic, eating dust. Hollywood, yeah."

"A fife?"

"Why not a high-rise, a penthouse off Fifty-ninth Street, the way it should be, throwing grand parties for all the power makers and shakers, movie stars, hell, the celebrities. You know what I'm talking about, Third, rocks stars and nobodies, and I could wear a bell gown"—he thinks she means a ball gown, looking over at her with her eyes shut as she holds her arms up in front of her now, her feet scrunching in the sand as though she were dancing while lying there, wriggling on the towel, her skin glistening—"like Vivien Leigh in *Gone with the Wind*. Of course, it would have to be crimson. Shit, with all our crazy amounts of money why isn't it like that? What are we doing? This is pure insanity."

"Of course, crimson."

"We ought to have an outdoor dance floor, a giant gazebo where a forty-piece orchestra plays classical pieces all night: Pachelbel's

*Canon* and Handel's *Concerto Grosso Number Six* and Bach's *Overture Number Three in Air*."

"With lots of fifes."

"We'd have horses and carriages. Yes, raising champagne glasses with me in a midnight toast to the beginning of a new year, new lives. And after, getting the timing down right, just a couple of minutes before dawn . . . a handsome stranger, in black, is standing there in the rose of the rising sun, knowing my every move before I do, a sort of half smirk on his face, his strong hands gesturing. The virile son of a bitch pulls me up off my diamond high heels, we do a fandango, my hair sweeping the floor as he dips me. . . ."

"Do they dip in the fandango?"

"And then we rush for his carriage, and he whips his horses into a frenzy as the sun bursts over the mountains, the horses shrieking down the road and we chase the fading gloom. . . ."

Strange, how it begins, with someone else's dreams, another's hate.

Joseph snaps forward, and brings his tremendous fists slapping down against the water, startling Rachel into silence. He digs his hands into the silt and scoops up heaps of mud, flinging them about wildly. It's a sign of impotence, but the frenzy is always a shock to behold. There's something terrifying but oddly reassuring in his menace, finally seeing all the roiling rage bleed out. His voice is full of all that's been invisible before: passion, heartache, breakdown.

"In my heart of hearts I wish you'd shut the fuck up!" he screams.

Rachel grins. Almost nothing can stop her from showing that wry mockery in her face. She's so gorgeous, but it's a painful sight, full of portent. Mud keeps flying. She's ready to lock horns, her teeth showing now as the grin widens to a leer, into a reckless smile. She's vehement, but not curious, as she asks, "And what is your problem?"

Jacob begs, "Quiet."

"Shut up, you."

Now, drawing his legs out of the water, his flaccid and nearly useless penis draped, as if it, too, is scowling at her, Joseph says, "You're a little girl, with these futile fantasies. Orchestras and the East Village, rock stars, movie sets—you sound like a goddamn imbecile when you talk this shit. And tell me this; just how in the fuck are you supposed to dance the fandango in a *goddamn bell gown?*"

"And you, what do you know? What suddenly makes you an expert on anything except being an imbecile, tough guy?"

"Nothing, I know nothing."

"There you go." Her lips form a pout, the muscles of her face folding, that vertical slash between her pollen-laden eyebrows crumbling her malice into a frown. Not much sport in this; the game over already, so soon? "Well, that's just wonderful, that's an impressive comeback."

"Fuck you."

"Oh, you must take such pride in that."

"Shut up."

"You shut up."

Jacob sighs and tries to add a soothing tone as she slides closer to him, her naked backside rubbing into his thigh, the sweat of her shoulders filled with radiance like diamonds. His mouth is open but none of his father's wisdom prevails, only a bitter silence. Rachel stands and looks down at Joseph with a well-practiced glare of derision, and then dives into the pond. She splashes less than usual, hardly making a ripple or disturbing the fish that loiter on the verge of the shore, watching the three of them intently.

Joseph says, "That bitch."

For no reason he can comprehend, without any emotion or direction or even intent, Jacob spits at his brother.

"You little fucking prick." His brother's

hand is iron, as always, as Jacob tries to scramble away in the dirt but isn't nearly fast enough. Grabbing him by the soft flesh between the branch of his neck and shoulder, fingers digging, digging further, Joseph grips hard onto the collarbone and hauls him forward with one mighty pull. Jacob screams; his throat and body are so full of pain that the screech is closed off, and he merely cringes and gapes.

Joseph wrenches him even closer, his other hand reaching around to grab Jacob by the ankle. The hatred that's always been palpable has finally taken form in action. His brother is a dragon awakened. Joseph's chest muscles ripple like animals coming alive under the skin, as he lifts his baby brother over his head like so much paper, twisting him, shredding him, and, with a shrug, he heaves Jacob ten feet out into the water like throwing him in the wastebasket.

In the air, finally released, he feels nothing for a moment, awaiting the cool touch of the inviting water. Abruptly, he strikes a wall of agony, and feels bone on bone as he lands on top of Rachel, whose beautifully smiling face has just broken the surface.

The green is exquisite, blinding, and much colder than before.

## The Deceased

Blood spurts into the pond.

Veins of crimson thread the water. His nose is smashed, but the greater amount of blood is pouring from his sister's mouth. He's read about people whose broken nose bones slide up into their brains, and he feels shards there, wondering if his cerebrum has been punctured. Stars and migraine lightning flashes are all he can see, no longer able to tell which direction is up. He swims the wrong way, kicking awkwardly, his limbs enmeshed with Rachel's. Trying to hold his breath, he's also talking to her, air bubbling from his mouth, and he doesn't know what he wants to say as he dives deeper, sinking. Her hair follows and traps him. He snaps free like fending off strands of silk, as she's dragged down into his drowning.

The red floats in front of his face like the swirling of Rachel's dream gown. He hiccups now, still speaking, and spots her clouding mouth working as well, bubbles and blood everywhere in the green. He wheels aside and brushes her torn lips with his cheek, ears popping. He thinks how perfect this would be under other circumstances, and the awful burning in his lungs bites and chews voraciously.

Joseph's hands finally come down for him,

sinewy torso towing those thin, ugly, crippled legs behind him, tugging again on that sensitive spot of Jacob's clavicle. He thinks he squeals again, a white-hot spear point driving hard into his forehead, and Rachel's voice is clear in his mind.

They stare at one another, all three of them, as a calmness descends like all his sister's hair pressed gently over his eyes.

There are seconds too long to be only seconds.

You add together those things that need to be added together: the panic and mutant fluids slithering forward to the temporal lobe, eldritch moments of flesh and blood meeting in the heart of wrath and sex magic. The black depths of the pond call to you as if they want what you symbolize more than yourself. Jacob understands his position in the scale of nature, in this instant. Rachel with her hand on his ankle, Joseph a murderous savior, the three of them descending . . .

. . . as he touches the fish.

They all scream, and it's an amazing sound, this far down in the water. A blaze and a burning, as Jacob's hands clench and unclench, feeling himself fading like Rachel's virile lover escaping in his carriage. The edge of that blade meeting the back of his head saws through memories, dredging up foolish elements that don't belong to him: he thinks of the East Village and a *bell* gown, oh, and somewhere there is a kinky hooker with wrinkles in the corners of her mouth who wants to roll across the floor. There is provocation here in the pond with them.

At last Rachel kicks awkwardly, and Joseph's massive arm slices upward; they almost break the surface, but not quite, not enough buoyancy with Jacob only dead weight, those feeble legs clacking him in the busted nose. They're in trouble. She's still out of it, and Joseph's one arm around them is loosening its grip, the other cutting overhead, using his frantic and power strokes to reach for air. But something else is happening, moving with them as if it *is* them.

Joseph's rickety kneecaps continue thunking Jacob in the face, keeping time with his pulse as the last few bubbles of his life float out of his nose and mouth. Alive still, somehow, he can barely make out the whites of his sister's eyes, rolled back in her head. He can barely feel the appalling abruptness of his erection and immediate—*what's that?*—ejaculation, his first, and cannot guess that around his fingertips an infinitesimal amount of water is boiling. The fish's gills spread wide

and stay open—it looks like a carp, perhaps—
tail whipping side to side, also in Jacob's face
until, dwindling rapidly, the tail is no more.
Rachel's hair floats down in a slow billowing
from above, and yet, impossibly, another
woman's tresses, white and with a green hue
in the pond, are moving toward him up from
below. Someone jerks on his foot, now gently
moving fingertips up his leg, nearing his inner
thigh, and his penis.

He snorts air as he breaks the surface,
awareness wrestling with unconsciousness.
Euphoria mingles with terror, as his sperm
and blood mix in the water.

Death and God seem nearby, but not nearly
close enough to help him breathe. The fists
are on his chest, pounding, always pummeling, beating the hell out of him again.

"Come on, you little pain in the ass."

He is breathing, but Joseph just likes to hit
him. His brother is lying in the mud like a
worm beside him, thumping Jacob's ribs, not
pressing down on his lungs. Rachel leans over
him, too, her breasts in his face, and he smiles
despite the fact that her blood rings her
mouth, now his, too, as she seals her lips over
his and kisses him, blowing air. She pinches
his swollen nose and the agony drives further
into his head. She tilts his neck back to an

even more painful angle, her tongue mashed against his own. He wants to say *Quit kissing me*, but he doesn't want to say it. His balls are oddly warm and sensitive. He feels a tightness in his throat, bile and silt rising, and has to turn over on his bad side to vomit, such a stew coming up.

Joseph's remote grimace fractures inch by inch, tears welling. There's not much sorrow though, and Jacob wipes his sister's blood from his lips. Sitting up, he gazes over the water, squinting into the sun as Rachel smoothes his hair back, rubbing his forehead and trying to get him to lie back down. "Relax, don't move."

He keeps searching. "Someone's out there."

"What?"

"In the water."

"There's nobody out there."

He doesn't know how the transition was made, but they're even more bound now, the three of them. He feels pity for his brother, and even a greater longing for his sister, having been in the carriage. "Something's happened."

"You're fine; we're all fine."

Rachel titters nervously, massaging his back and lightly scratching his skin, gingerly touching him now as if he, or she, might break apart under any more pressure. She brushes crust from her mouth, nodding absently. Joseph pulls himself to a seated position in the dirt and holds those lethal fists out, making futile gestures to his siblings. "I—"

"Shut the fuck up," Rachel says.

"He's right," Joseph says.

"Just get into your chair and let's get the hell out of here. He's probably got a concussion."

"He's right; something did happen."

"Come on, come on . . . let's just go . . ."

Jacob attempts to get to his feet and amazes himself by doing so. He scans the water as Rachel drapes her arms over his shoulders, tugging him backward, guiding him away from the shore. "Get dressed; let's go."

"We've got to stay," he insists. "Someone's out there. Didn't either of you see her?"

"Nobody's out there!" she hisses.

"You had to have seen her."

"I saw her," Joseph says, and the wind is a perfect counterpoint to his voice. Rachel stumbles back a step and shudders. He's so covered with mud he doesn't look quite human anymore, like a corpse freshly dug up, and with all the same dead emotion in his eyes. He peers into the forest, searching, looks back at the water as the thick trails of blood eke toward them inch by inch. He's unable to keep his gaze set on any one given spot for a length of time, and Jacob follows his brother's line of sight with each swivel of his head.

And before another word can be said, or any answers found, further insults made . . . before Rachel's battered lips continue veering into a terrified snarl and Jacob's eye can catch the glinting yellow slits watching him . . . before they can move away or shout . . . even before they can grab hold of one another, the three of them who have made this moment happen, Ophelia is there, their dream a reality, his muse come to life, rising from the pond.

Dripping.

Water swirls down from her back, long hair curled aside to show off the lovely yet remotely fishlike visage. Rachel gasps and strikes the same pose. Their siren isn't nearly as confused as they are. Born in the maelstrom, she is of it. Who wouldn't die or murder for her . . . aquatic curves of that body promising unbelievable mobility, as she smiles. Dripping. That's Joseph's image, the long wet hair, the beads of water easing down to hang eternally off a hard nipple.

Joseph growls a command, though not distinct enough to be understood. The woman from the water steps toward them with embers blazing in that yellow glare, the same sensual wrinkles around her mouth as his one and only lover.

The attitude of authority Rachel has always held drains from her face until only minutiae remains. She actually swoons as if the dance is done, the carriage awaiting her that will pave the way of escape. Frozen to his spot, Jacob can't move to his sister, can't run and isn't sure he wants to; he's looking only at himself and his family. Her name presents itself clearly to him, plucked from his father's library: *Ophelia*. There is nothing to be frightened of anymore. How clearly they see themselves and each other. Rachel lets out a bark of laughter that makes him drop to his knees.

He says, "God," but it's not enough of an invocation, much weaker than the magic at work here. Ophelia is of them, gazing lovingly at Jacob and reaching down for his hand. He allows her to touch him and nearly giggles because she's so warm, so soft, like Rachel's breasts in the sun. Joseph is silent now, yet leering and still somehow laughing, crawling forward to the coiling of this flesh. Jacob can't believe what it is he's bearing witness to as his brother pulls Rachel down slowly, so much more tenderly than should be possible for him, until she is with him in the dirt, still stunned but beginning to smile now, too. He thinks he might vomit and then knows he won't. There's a twitching in his forehead. Ophelia leads Jacob to the heart of this earth, nipping and naming him, while his siblings, caught up in the game again and laughing loudly, so much high-pitched giggling near his ear, begin to moan and start calling him Lucifer. Yes, calling him Moreau.

# *Chapter Seventeen*

He remembered.

Ophelia placed a webbed hand over her distended belly and said, "A son or daughter, which do you prefer?"

Jacob scrambled up the shore and made for the house, unable to feel anything except the all-consuming horror that was himself.

Thrashing, there was always the thrashing.

In the hospital especially. Anxious ladies on

the ward would scream into their sheets in the middle of the night, calling for their husbands, their children, shrieking their fathers' names, all the while flinging pillows and killing people with clawhammers in their dreams. Attendants were always rushing in with medication, these big-ass needles, pills that would choke a goat, and calming words that sounded so static but sincere. For a moment you almost didn't realize how hollow it all was, how it didn't even pertain to you because they had no idea what really went on. She'd been strapped down only once, and it had been enough for her to keep the welling pain inside her and not show it anymore, because if you showed too much of its face the nurses couldn't handle it. They'd simply try to kill the baby again, even the memory of the baby, because it was too great a burden even for these strangers.

In a sleepy slow-motion she jerked sideways again, the nightmare so real and intense, clear and yet somehow undefined, while she struggled in bed. Violently rolling she slipped off the mattress like a seal sliding down a rock, tumbling out of bed in a tangle of blankets but landing on her feet, already standing.

"Jesus . . ."

She'd seen a woman die once, in the hospital.

A nurse by the name of Olivetti, who was always talking about her grandchildren and their spouses and the rest of what must have been an immense and exacting brood. Olivetti did it all, kept the show afloat. Turned on the lights in the morning and clicked them off at night, waving to them all, handed out the mail, administered enemas, hugged the weeping, taught some of the others how to play chess, once even fixed the cracked plaster of D wing, where a girl with buckteeth had gnawed it in a fit of mania. Katie kept her distance. Olivetti was adorable and beautiful but with a large, looming intensity for love that could hurt you if you weren't ready for it, like throwing a spotlight on somebody who'd been lying in shadows too long. Katie had never seen anyone smile so much, or laugh with her giant jugs bouncing around but not a hint of self-consciousness. Olivetti died sort of smiling, giving an enema to a new girl, Sarah, who liked to yell at the television. Sarah enjoyed enemas and asked for them regularly, and since the medication had her pretty backed up most of the time, Olivetti obliged on occasion. That woman died of a massive heart attack, thrashing, twisting for about two minutes while everybody raced around yelling, and Sarah's taut, naked ass with a tube halfway inserted witnessed the final grimacing breaths of a gurgling, kind woman.

Fumbling for the lamp, Katie became instantly aware of her surroundings. Nice to come out of it and not find yourself trapped in any kind of dream fugue. The lamp skirted along the edge of the nightstand, and she quickly set it right. Lisa shuffled the covers, mattress springs groaning as she sat up in bed. Katie waited a moment, hoping Lisa would go back to sleep, but she kept hearing the same rustling of cloth, the squeaking getting louder now. Was she masturbating? The movements slowed, bed frame crackling with the shifting of weight as Lisa sat up, too, now fumbling about.

Katie turned on the light and said, "Sorry I woke you, had a nasty dream."

She stared into the face of a woman she'd never seen before.

"Now, please go," the lady implored kindly, but with an intense frown. "You've got to go, Kathleen; you must leave my son alone." So lovely, motherly in a way that Katie's mother never was. "I'm not sure if he can bring himself back. Listen to me; I'm trying to help you."

Katie was listening all right.

Because the woman's eyelids seemed to be shriveling, turning black with words scrawled on them like tattoos, always changing, running over the skin. So slowly, though, with everything happening as if the air had turned to sand, so that Katie had to lean forward to see what was actually occurring. Amazingly, she reached out as though she wanted to grab the woman's face, turn it aside, have her shut her eyes so that Katie could read the sentences running over them. She said, "What?" Her voice was so whiny and diminutive it was like Minnie Mouse. "What?" It made her giggle, but the woman just glared wildly. Yes, the lady's eyes turned red, her ears curling in a strange fashion, everything becoming bloody now, with capillaries exploding. The flesh of her skull split in an odd pattern, as if there were a reason for it occurring in just the manner it did, so that you could almost read more words in the cracks of her blistered skin. Her cheeks crawled and receded further, her gray hair coming off in charred clumps to litter the pillow, throwing sparks and wafting into the air, slowly drifting over to Katie. That friendly woman's face, tacky like wet paint, was melting off.

But at least the face was connected to the head.

The head wasn't connected to anything.

# *Chapter Eighteen*

Her toes caught in the spokes of the wheel, as if it actually fought back, moving in front of her on its own accord, bopping and weaving, she tripped and felt the rear metal bar strike her brutally in the belly. Taking a couple of seconds to think about the baby, she wondered if the other versions of Lisa everywhere else were relieved, or grinning, or weeping—just as hands strong enough to snap granite snatched her out of the air.

She wondered if the other Lisa following her all this time had finally caught up, and if so, who she might possibly turn to now. She tried to shout for Katie again, but the arms held her too tightly; this Lisa must've been *really* pissed off. She couldn't catch her breath, feeling her face going red, then white, cold sweat exploding onto her forehead. The world went concentric, starting a slow spin that sped up rapidly, and Lisa realized that the choking *glck* sounds were coming from her. Abruptly the hands released her, brushing hair back from around her ear. A deep and indifferent voice behind her commanded, "Relax."

She dropped to her knees, gasping heavily, holding on to the wheelchair for support. She wanted to curse somebody out but nothing came up. The hands stayed with her, massaging her shoulders with a callous touch. She couldn't see a face yet, but knew it wasn't Jacob. Maybe the cops were here, having finally figured out he'd killed them all, and were ready to make an arrest after ten years. Whoever he might be, he shoved her a bit to one side, as if enjoying the feel of her body's resistance, and brushed hard against her breast, let it wobble, then brought his hand against it once more. She stood into a half crouch and turned to look at him.

Another *glck* noise as she coughed, surprised to see that she'd somehow made it into the parlor, never having found any staircase. It seemed impossible that the loops and coils had taken her through the course of the corridors. God, after that, how would she ever find Katie?

He laughed again.

A man built of total poise as well as solid muscle leered at her, and she knew she was in trouble now. If he was a cop he wasn't here to solve anything, but maybe had been in on a cover-up, all this money going to set some killer free. He was obviously a bodybuilder. Jesus, he had the kind of neck that always turned her on, and even now she couldn't help but admire him. His biceps appeared determined to rip their way from his shirt. He stared at her with a cocky, greasy confidence that bled from his schoolboy grin, and she knew she was in deep shit, seriously deep fucking shit.

"Um . . ."

"Hello," he said. "You're warm."

What the fuck did that mean? What to throw him? The charm, the nasty scowl and righteous anger? "Um . . ."

Appetite designed his smile. He raised his

hand, maybe to hit her or maybe not, and got distracted, glancing at his own palm. He seemed absorbed, and licked his hand as if licking her.

A teenage girl sat on the couch behind them, sporting a sneer of her own, and held her hands out and clapped a couple of times. "Nice entrance, Red. Ever consider aerial-wire walking?"

"No," Lisa said.

"Well, that's a damn shame."

Nodding, she went with the flow. "Isn't it, though."

Lisa wavered, her legs rubbery, still feeling lost in the house even with the front door right over there. The girl laid herself out a bit more seductively on the couch, her summer dress lifting inch by inch as she shifted across the cushions, showing off a stunning pair of legs. The guy quit laughing and that was worse, crossing his immense arms over that enormous chest, both of them getting way too comfy. The atmosphere grew more and more intense with all kinds of rushes, and for all the bustling force she wondered if she could ever get away and make her way back to Katie, if one or two more screams might bring help running in from someplace. The room pulsed with rape.

"Who are you? Where's Jacob?"

The girl got up and kind of pranced around. She had the healthy swagger of someone with great sexual capacity and longevity. Lisa had it, too. The girl moved stealthily to the fireplace, tilting portraits of the Maelstroms and letting them swing back and forth like pendulums, allowing the intricately carved frames to clack loudly into one another in a cloud of dust. "He didn't mention having any company this weekend, so who are you, Red?"

"A friend."

"Jacob doesn't have friends."

"So who are you then?"

"He should have told you. Who are you, Red?"

Damn, that kind of self-assurance could sure be off-putting. One of those people who kept repeating things, called you "snookie" or "sparky" just to get under your skin. Lisa's eyes darted, looking for a weapon. She could see no little stand full of pokers and other shit by the fireplace; everyone knew you went for that first. Where else did you check? The umbrella stand, like you might hit them upside the head with one. Most of the furniture remained covered in sheets; she couldn't even tell if there was a vase or ashtray handy. The dust made her want to sneeze again, and she fought it off, her mouth widening, all of a sudden squinting and trying to hold it in as the tears came, and then the fit of sneezing followed.

They knew who she was already. She understood that they knew, but said it anyway. "I'm Lisa."

"Of course you are, Lisa," he said, enjoying how ill at ease he set her with his powerful presence. He moved forward and back as if corralling her in the space between himself, the girl, and the wheelchair. "Sorry if we startled you. My name is Joseph, and this is my sister, Rachel."

"Hello, Lisa," Rachel said, taking the portraits down now and throwing them into the fireplace.

"What the hell do you think you're doing?" Lisa asked.

"Cleaning up," Rachel said.

"That's cute."

"Do you think so?"

All right, so what to do, and how to do it without mentioning Katie? Play like Jacob's lover. Would that give her an edge, or make her more of a target? Was that the problem here? Had she walked into some kind of tumultuous affair, all this bad blood so apparent that she could almost see a crusty pool of it on the floor?

"And what are you doing here, Lisa?" Joseph asked.

"I work for Jacob's agent."

"Isn't that funny," he said, no hint of humor at all in his manner. "I bumped into Robert a few nights ago and he never mentioned having a secretary."

"Neither did I. I just said I worked for him."

"He did mention his lovely new girlfriend though."

Okay, so they were moving out into the open now, a little less subtle and calculated. She wondered just where it would stop, exactly when she should run, which direction, where the hell the pokers were. "You're lying," she said calmly. "You two sure like to play together."

"Am I? Lying, I mean?" He tilted his head, thinking about it, as if he actually had to put some effort into it, not even aware of what he was saying. "Do we? Play lots of games?"

Rachel gave a slim-hipped sway, as if she needed to break into a slow dance but didn't want to jump the gun just yet. "Yes, we know how to play together."

"Give me a break. Where's Jacob?"

Rachel shrugged, and even that gesture

proved to be graceful. "We don't know; we only just got here ourselves."

"Uh-huh."

A seal-like bark from the big guy, who kept up the leer.

"Is he writing?" Rachel continued, almost on her toes, as if she wanted to move into a ballet. "Up in his father's study, hoping a little of the talent will rub off? You don't read their stuff, do you? I can tell. None of that wildfire in your eye, like you just had your warlock hunter McNellis of Ariovagne books signed. They go for about three-fifty at conventions, or used to anyway. Jacob likes the study. As if the power were in the typewriter, a battery storing Dad's genius. You think that's where he is? Not like he'd be doing anything else now, would he? He hasn't done anything else for ten years. It's awful for him, of course, the way the solitude traps him. But he prefers just being a silhouette; anyone can see that. Your friend knows that."

*Ah, fuck.* So they knew about Katie, too, and just how long had they been watching? Had they been out there in the woods, camped beside them when they'd been stuck looking for the bridge?

"Where is he?" Lisa said, feeling the two of them dancing around her even when they weren't moving. Something bad had been done to piss these two off, and she didn't want to get stuck taking any heat because of a guy she hardly knew who was probably a psycho himself.

"I don't know," Rachel said.

Backing up a step, Lisa hit the spokes again. "What was the wheelchair doing in the hall?"

Dropping the smile, the grin, his leer, Joseph froze his face into a guise about as expressionless an expression as she'd ever seen in her life. "Who can tell? Guess it belonged to someone who used to live here. I think one of them was crippled. I think he died a cripple."

"Yes," she said.

"Yes, I'm sure of it."

Wandering over to her brother, Rachel smoothed his back, the same way that he'd touched Lisa's back, really rubbing, enjoying the feel of muscle underneath. No sincerity in them whatsoever except for the anger and distinctly careless attitude of the domineering and corrupt who are completely in control. How far down did it go?

Rachel pressed closer to her brother—if that was what he was, and he couldn't be, just look, as she kissed his neck with a trailing tongue. Her arms entwined around him, slinky as a cat with that perfect teenage suppleness, so sleek and lithe. Lisa had lost that about two years ago, kept thinking of how her tits would sag if she went through with having the kid.

Joseph said, "You're warm." Turning to Lisa and smiling again, his teeth so white they seemed to glow, he looked genuinely enthralled. "She's warm." They started kissing passionately, embracing madly, like they were gonna do it on the floor right in front of her now.

"Uhhh . . ." She was in the serious fucking deep shit of the septic world all right, and started backing out of the parlor, inch by inch, hardly even lifting her feet but just kind of moonwalking along the carpet, easing herself out. She looked down at the fireplace, hoping not to make contact with anything, to slip out without being noticed really, as the two of them started fondling one another in earnest, kissing even more intensely, cheek to cheek, caressing each other's neck and fingers combing through hair. Rachel kept her tongue out with a bawdy smile thick with sex, licking and giggling with heinous meaning. Like his body was cut from rock, he stood stolid as she moved down his body, touching his legs almost daintily, then gripping his thighs, her hand moving easily and with extreme familiarity over his crotch.

Lisa thought about all the times her father had yelled at her to start carrying a gun, and how she'd argued with the old man.

Joseph wheeled, not having forgotten about her. "Anything wrong?" he asked.

"No, of course not, nothing at all."

"You look a little tired. It's late. Don't let us keep you."

Rachel didn't let up the eye contact at all, or the dancing, or the touching. *Those are Jacob's eyes.* "Oh, come on. Let's keep her."

This was how it got sometimes, on the bad nights when she knew that no matter how much she knew about how the world worked or how well she got along with people, or how sexy she could shake it or how fast she could talk, there was no way to get clear of the rapidly approaching entrance of hell.

"Screw this shit!" Lisa said.

She turned and ran.

Straight into the wheelchair.

She flipped over and onto it, the left side of her head coming down hard against the uncushioned armrest. Her back slammed across the seat at a bad angle, with an audible crackling. A heated spike of agony sheared through her. The wheelchair moved forward, with Lisa in it like a sack of meat, rolling toward them as they stood waiting and smiling. Bent over like this, her ass hiked into the air, arms splayed, knee pressed upward near her chest, she tasted the blood as it ran down her forehead into her mouth. She tried to move and couldn't, the nerves in her back running a fiery electrical tremor up into her neck, but that was all.

She heard screaming, but it wasn't her own. You were always supposed to get confused about that, like you didn't know where it was coming from. She whimpered, ribbons of blood hanging from her lips, listening to Katie shriek.

Finally the unyielding metal took a little pity and let her go. She slumped over, gravity drawing her into an amazingly slow, arching spin that abruptly ended when she hit the floor. She grunted as even more pain fired through the top of her neck, blazing white-hot directly into the back of her skull. Her jaw ached, too, as she landed in a heap with her head tilted up, her chin grinding violently into the floor. The two of them were perfectly framed in her vision.

Joseph and Rachel, naked, but with no clothes to be seen on the floor or anyplace else. The girl so slinky and knowing it, stretching, each step a performance of acrobatics as she approached. He followed her, reaching for her hand, both of them slithery with every movement. Stealing across the floor in carefully posed eroticism, they stood in front of Lisa now, just looking down.

Her blood kept leaking over her teeth, pooling around her chin. Rachel knelt and wrapped herself around her brother's ankles, reaching up to touch his erection, kissing him, her tongue all over, working his legs especially. He got a real kick out of that. Lisa tried to turn her head again and failed again, struggling to move and managing the smallest of crawls.

Katie continued screaming. Jacob must be up there chasing her around with an ax. Lisa's shoulder slid an inch or two toward them, then stopped as she tried to reverse herself, but the crackling came on so loud there at the base of her neck again that she gurgled and mewled, hating the desperate sound of it.

She tried to control herself but started crying.

"Aw," Joseph said.

Rachel tittered, still working him with her hands, her mouth.

Lisa spotted movement in the corner of the

213

room, by the front door, and hoped it would be Jacob with his father's shotgun, standing there stuffed full of that calm demeanor. Maybe he wasn't crazy at all, but just biding his time, about to rush in and save the day. He wouldn't bother wasting time talking, trying to figure the whole scene out. Those eyes would see the portraits in the fireplace and that would mean more to him than Lisa drooling and crying at the foot of the wheelchair. No, just pulling the trigger, getting it done in a heartbeat.

The turtle, easing across the floor, stared back at her.

Joseph dropped beside Lisa, and ran his hands through her hair, pulling it up to his face, where he smothered himself in those scarlet locks, now sucking on the strands, chewing. He reached down and took firm hold of her breasts, pulling them roughly as he ripped open her shirt. He apparently found her bra deeply affecting, simply scratching lightly at the cups, as if he'd never seen one before.

He looked into her eyes and said, "You're warm."

Rachel raised herself up, her limbs so fluid

that there seemed to be no bones as she surged forth, crawling atop Lisa.

Fingers probed, and the turtle stalked closer.

# *Chapter Ninteen*

Since she was screaming, maybe the time had finally come to think about Grandpa.

Or maybe not, she couldn't tell beneath the scrutiny of the dead woman's melting face.

It seemed like such a clumsy way to go after a person: you heave the ax way up high into the air, both arms overhead, and by the time you yank the blade back down the person has had plenty of time to scramble away. But somehow, no . . . none of them had made it.

Katie hadn't thought much about her grandfather since the hospital, and in there it hadn't been for any of the reasons she would have expected. In the bed next to her sat a woman who did little besides mutter novenas and count "Our Fathers" off her rosary beads. At first the constant mumbled prayers barely broke into Katie's sedated existence, but after a few days the woman's muffled chants became a living pressure of sorts, a kind of cycle of anxiety as the words repeated, finished, and began again, endlessly. Soon Katie could think of nothing else, not even the baby, enthralled by the woman's ability to never become distracted, not even for a moment, by whatever had driven her here from the husband and two kids whom she never said a word to on visiting days. Each prayer complete in its perfection . . . but . . . but . . .

. . . she still wasn't thinking about her grandfather.

Really, she had started slowly recalling him in the hospital by getting into the memories from Nana's end, because Nana had said the rosary, too, by rote, of course, like all of them, and without much interest, fumbling the lines. Every few months, Katie would sleep over her grandparents' house in Red Hook and just watch television and wait for her father to pick her up again. Sometimes she and Grandpa went to the zoo—the man talking to her without any enthusiasm, as bored as she was, both of them forced into this pattern simply because they had somehow, inexplicably, been placed here together, both still wondering how and why, and what they might do about it.

He stood barely five foot five, a little on the stocky side, with a grin that made him look serene—a smile of great complexity that took over entire portions of his face. You could see happiness in certain sections, hidden inside the patchwork, woven in there among all the melancholy. Grandma, also petite, had a mouth that hung too low on the left, showing off more of her ill-fitting dentures on that side. They both wore glasses with solid metal frames—her grandfather's lenses didn't really change his appearance much, but Nana's gave the upper part of her face a strange, elongated cast, as if part of her head were actually taffy gradually being pulled.

In Ozone Park he'd been a shoemaker, what he called a cobbler. He'd retired early but still made lots of shoes: beautifully crafted ones for the men in the family, and oddly thick, tight ones for Katie that never seemed to scuff or wear in.

## Tom Piccirilli

There were knives around to cut the leather and fine-tool the soles. The doctors had asked her about her grandfather and she'd replied: "He was a sweet man. He made shoes." They asked about her grandmother and she'd said, "My Nana is dead." The doctors didn't seem completely satisfied, having heard the history from her mother, but strangely they disregarded it for the most part, barely dipping back into it, but harped about Tim and the baby for hours on end.

Nana had statues of Christ and saints you never heard about all over the house, palms from Palm Sunday shaped into crosses that rustled at the touch, different crucifixes on the walls depicting various contortions of Christ. Katie was fascinated by their differences—some of them had him openmouthed, even crying, the paint fresh and red and running from the wounds. Others portrayed him as nearly sleeping, not in any pain, the blood placed efficiently in the creases and holes, as if the sculptor had tried to conserve his supplies.

Nana would get migraines, take off her glasses and rub her eyes, and Katie would get her cold compresses and try to make up good answers that didn't sound stilted when her grandmother said, "Tell me how things are going for you in school, honey." Nana would seem attentive while Katie talked about homework and ballet class and violin lessons. Katie needed about seven minutes' worth of material before Nana's mouth drooped open and the old woman fell soundly asleep.

Her grandparents whispered and sometimes giggled at night, listening to music in another language. Nana's laughter occasionally seemed contrived, and at other times sounded like a grunt of amused despair. Grandpa sometimes chuckled with a noise that made Katie smile, right up to the last second when it would abruptly break into a groan. Katie had heard them crying together once or twice. If they did it on her sporadic visits, how often did they weep when alone?

That last morning, when she awoke to find him standing over her bed, Grandpa had begun with an apology, pulling her small suitcase from the corner where it always sat on these weekends, and started packing her clothes for her, doing an awful job.

She checked the clock. "My dad won't be here until eleven."

Grandpa nodded and said that he knew, he knew, and kept packing, but he couldn't make it all fit correctly. She got dressed quickly and repacked her belongings, glad that she was going to leave early today and not have to go back to the zoo, where Grandpa really only liked to watch the monkeys screw and throw their shit out at the crowd. He told her to go sit outside and wait for her father, kissed her on top of the head, which was kissing her hair—she hated that but he always did it—then led her to the brick porch with the rusted overhang. She sat waiting with her suitcase beside her, relieved she had broken at least part of the pattern today. She didn't have to hug Grandma, or get kissed on the bridge of her nose while looking into those stretched, magnified eyes. Maybe it would be better next time.

Amazing how quickly everything inside could turn, moving from one emotion to the next. Katie held out for about twenty minutes, bored on the porch and not quite sure what had led her here, almost wishing she were at the zoo and the monkeys were pissing off the crowd. At least there she could get to see some cute boys. She soon grew sick of the fact that every car coming down the street was not her father's, and felt too uncovered, out in the open like this.

Grandpa had locked the door but hadn't completely shut it: the wood of the jamb had rotted and been inexpertly fixed and painted time and again, screws and nails sticking out too far, so that the lock and knob jiggled.

The doctors didn't want her to mention most of this; they wanted her to start right here, when they wanted her to talk about it at all, which she never did.

Katie entered, feeling ashamed in a fashion, as if she'd been offered the chance to break the cycle but had somehow slipped up in the escape, willfully reentering into the circuit. She called out, "My father isn't here yet."

She thought she heard some kind of response, which prompted her to the bedroom.

The doctors always asked, "What, what did you hear?" and she couldn't remember if she'd heard anything. They all thought she was repressing something and kept after it. "What, what, what," like the cackling of crows.

Nana lay on the bed, with her dentures jutting from her mouth, the bottom set resting on her chin and the upper set angled as if she were about to bite into a huge apple. One eyeglass lens was cracked, the other lying on the floor intact. Katie stared, taking in the image of Nana like this: the sleeve of her dress torn a little, a thin trail of pink froth drying on her top lip, splashes of blood on her chest and stomach. Her steps became smaller, her feet in her tight shoes, but she kept proceeding forward, entranced by her grandmother's one open eye, which looked so normal now without the lens protracting her face. So ordinary yet almost pretty, despite the fact that Nana was so dead.

The barely audible sound of dripping brought her attention to the bathroom. She felt no fear, not even too great a curiosity, as she pressed the door wide.

Her shoes squeaked on the tile.

The shrinks expected more. They wanted a meaty story of incest and child abuse, to hear about Grandpa chasing her around trying to have sex with her, but the old guy couldn't even get out of the way of the shit the monkeys sometimes tagged him with.

Grandpa had cut his wrists and done a good job of it: the left had been opened nice and wide, but the right, Jesus, he'd put a lot into it, and nearly sawed completely through. He was still wearing his clothes, which looked dyed red from the crimson water. He panted, his chest moving rapidly, and turned his head aside to look at her.

Of course, he'd wanted to have their corpses be found, but they had no friends, no phone calls, no visitors—it might've taken weeks before anyone discovered them this way, perhaps Katie herself the next time she was meant to sleep over. He'd apologized to her earlier for his need, his fear, and had tried to warn her, packing her small bag, but Grandpa hadn't been able to control himself well enough. If only he'd waited until the appropriate time, when her father was outside, she would have been spared this sight, the sudden knowledge of the dire weaknesses she'd inherited. She continued watching in silence as he gave up his last breath and turned his face away from her in remorse, and his nose slowly sank under the water.

She waited there, straying back and forth from the bathroom to the bedroom for hours, but she couldn't remember having thought about anything.

And yet—and the shrinks really liked this part—once or twice a year since then, usually when she was ill with fever and just drifting off to sleep, she could feel the essence of her thoughts from those lost hours welling close enough for her to nearly grab hold of. She'd come closest to reaching it right there in the Ding-a-ling wing with the muttering woman beside her.

She didn't expect ever to find revelation or

even recognition, but simply an exhumation of that dead part of herself.

Jacob had been in the closet for three days, alone with his thoughts and the smell of blood and decaying bodies, and maybe that was part of what had brought her here.

Now, heading for the door, the woman's head no longer on Lisa's bed, Katie wondered if Nana would be found somewhere in this house. Or Grandpa.

Or Tim.

Or the baby.

She opened the door and went to look.

## *Chapter Twenty*

With every step closer to the house the drain-
ing grew worse, his soul torn into so many
directions at once, ripped by hands and
claws. Jacob heard different songs and en-
treaties on the island, sung by the dead, the
living, and now the screaming. Without fully
noticing, he passed through the front door
and drifted into the parlor.

Mom waited there by the stairs, holding
her hands out to him. How long had she been

trapped inside the maelstrom exactly like this? From the instant of her death? The moment she'd first met his father? Or even before that? Millennia weighed on all their shoulders. The four rivers were like those that encircled Eden: Pison, Gihon, Hiddekel, and the Euphrates. Was he Cain or Abel? And which of their sacrifices had been spurned by God?

He could almost see it as a scene from one of his own novels, where sons constantly sought out the myths of their parents, dramatic overtures made in the denouement, where resolution was hopefully found.

*Denouement isn't the end result,* his father had told him, pronouncing it a little off, going for a French-waiter accent with too much zeal, like *denoo-mint. From 'desnouer,' it means an untying of events following climax, in which such a clarification takes place. It's not where you knot the threads; this is where you loosen your hold on the reader so that they don't hate your guts for yanking them through hell and keeping them there afterward.*

Veins on his mother's hands bulged, as if she might grab hold of his chin and snap his neck.

"Get away from me," he said.

Fleshed-out forms of his brother and sister

slapped and straddled Lisa as she grimaced
and wailed beneath their fury. Jacob rushed
forward but could hardly feel even his own
presence anymore—each of these pressures
of the past and present collided within his lost
substance, turning him to dust. All that red
hair, he knew how it excited his siblings, who
had once begged for specifications of beauty,
size, color, and sharpness of teeth when
choosing the muses.

Lisa shrieked.

He wheeled, suddenly growling but not taking any breaths. "Stop them, Mother; you've
got to help me stop them. . . ."

Maybe she would. It at least seemed a possibility where so much else proved impossible. She stared down at him with an
expressionless gaze that subtly became more
human, her mouth tilting; she looked confused, perhaps, or merely impartial, a prod-
uct of the house. He stepped closer, passing
through Rachel, who snapped to attention as
if tickled and started laughing even louder.

He wondered if the hands of his mother
might finally release him. She worked her fingers over his forehead the way she'd done on
the awful nights when he'd called for her.
Only her soothing massages could help extin-
guish the blinding crush of his skull, as if she

mollified the extra growths and shards of bone in his brain. He reached to touch her skirt, bent as a boy can break down only before his own mother. Lying at her feet like a puppy, still growling and gritting his teeth, he wanted to feel the warmth from her that he hadn't felt in a decade. "I'm sorry," he said, and she almost appeared to make some *shusshhing* sounds. "I know it's always been my fault. . . ." No, he didn't, but he'd say anything now. "Help me. Stop them."

His mind whirled with the cold realization: *I'm dead. I'm dead, too.*

"You have been for a long time," Joseph called out, rising and leaving Lisa as he sauntered to the stairway. No . . . he swaggered over, throwing his hips and ass into the walk . . . a nearly effeminate sashay. The wheelchair roamed the room under its own will, circling the furniture and battering the walls. "You've never known what it meant to be alive."

Jacob tensed, staring through a tangle of hair that had fallen into his eyes, his mother trapped in her pattern and still kneading his temples. "Actually, I do," he said.

His sister joined in against him, of course, stroking Lisa's hair as the grinning kids and laughing parents in the picture frames leered from their family history. Where was the murder there? Should they have been able to notice? Had the signs been in them even then?

"It's not only out there," Rachel said, cocking a thumb at the window. "Your life and death. You always forgot about what went on in here, Third, what was happening right here."

So there it was, not even sounding evil anymore but merely frail and bitter, that he should have ever been in a position to judge them.

His sister's teeth snapped together the way they had in the woods when she grew excited. "And what kind of complexes are your biographers blaming on me, or him, or on them, when it's all your own fault?"

"Maybe that's true," he said, his voice nothing more than a hiss of draft flowing through the house. *Maybe.* He moved past Rachel, tried to hold on to one of Lisa's weakly flopping hands, but couldn't feel it. Bruises discolored her face, and blood ran from the sides of her mouth. A turtle rested in the red puddle, gazing solemnly at him as if wanting to ask a question.

Joseph laughed, throwing every bit of brutality into the guffaw and still coming up

231

short, and kicked the piano stool through his brother. "To think that you've been suicidal."

"Yes," Jacob said. "Just imagine."

"You made the dead your life."

"Something like that."

Wind buffeted the broken shutters, so that the rhythmic cracking of wood on wood gave them all a beat to move to. Joseph looked as though he wanted to twirl on his new legs, do the fox-trot, just keep moving. The rain thrashed again, once more striking the windows like the fists of scared children, as he heard his other lovers dancing and mewling, dangling from branches out in the forest, rolling in the brush.

"They want you," Rachel said.

"And you." *Yes, just imagine, think of the cost in soul when you are legion and there's so much blood and birthright on your hands.* "Beth?" he whispered, and thought of her in the closet, her beautiful pale face pressed against the crack of the door, her eyes glistening and peering as her mouth fell open and she begged, as always, to be let out of the shadows.

He thought of Katie too, and what could possibly be happening to her in the center of so much wrath. She knew something that he knew, or there'd be no reason for her to come after him the way she had. Jacob couldn't understand what it might be. He fell to his knees, being legion, feeling the *need* of his offspring, the rage of Rachel, the jealousy of Joseph, the loss of his mother, but feeling nothing of his own desires—if he'd ever had any.

He heard noise on the steps, and feared that he'd see their heads there, rolling down and out the front door, tongues lolling as they went spinning by. He realized they were footsteps coming down the stairs, one by one as he counted them, and didn't dare look up just yet.

As she sat beside him and pressed the heels of her palms against his forehead—sweaty hands that brought him some heat—with a gentleness he'd never quite believed existed, she rubbed lightly down the length of his neck. At once they were the hands of a wife, and he felt himself slowly being pulled from the pit. Rachel and Joseph grumbled unintelligibly behind him, but laughing still, as if they understood that this moment would eventually come. Their barbed hatred yanked him backward, but Katie managed to keep her grip on him. He couldn't understand how. Maybe if he'd loved her, if they had known each other more than a few hours, if he'd said something to her worthwhile instead of handing her only silence. So how could she make contact with him now, when nothing else could?

He could feel her desperation, her need to get down to Lisa, as she started crying and frantically tugging at him. "Get up! Wake up!"

She grabbed him by the shoulders—actually touching him, right there, his flesh tingling with live nerves again, uncongealed blood racing.

"You're warm," he said, and on the floor beneath them lay Lisa moaning, his brother and sister nowhere in sight.

Katie hugged him and pressed her cheek to his chest, helping him to stand. Slowly, with as much meaning as he'd ever put into any action or thought before, he kissed her, thinking, I might love you.

And thinking, Where are you, Dad?

# Chapter Twenty-one

Robert Wakely held the wineglass full of whiskey out in front of him, proffering it to death.

The figure of Isaac Maelstrom sitting on the couch opposite him solemnly waved the offer away.

Wakely shrugged and gulped another mouthful, not nearly drunk enough to believe he was drunk enough to be seeing this. "I sure do wish you'd tell me why you've come back,

Isaac. Your son went off to meet you and now you're here. It doesn't make much sense to me. I know there are unresolved issues. You had too many of them when you were alive not to still have them. I can't quite figure it out."

Isaac didn't comment, and most certainly didn't help him figure it out.

Waves crashed. Surf rifled up the sand toward the back door of the beach house. He loved to watch Lisa walking out there, in a dress, or bikini, or naked at midnight under the moon; he loved to watch her do anything.

Flashing lights caught Wakely's attention off to his left, in the kitchen; he spun but couldn't make anything out, squinted and glanced again. Through his stupor he finally saw that the answering machine flickered four times. He couldn't remember having heard the phone ring. Maybe it was Lisa calling to get in touch with him, to talk about his unresponsiveness lately. Christ, she was probably pissed.

He didn't want a kid.

He had become completely infested with alarm, terrified another kid would ever grow up to contain what was contained inside of Jacob Maelstrom.

Wakely hitched his pants and pressed the

button to replay the messages. After a moment of soft buzzing he realized the volume had been set too low. He shifted the dial to make it louder but hit the wrong button. The machine beeped angrily and shut off; he turned it back on again and accidentally slapped his outgoing message—"Hello, you've reached . . ."—cut it off and pressed the button to replay the incoming messages, and immediately understood that in the process he'd erased the four calls.

"Shit." He refilled his wineglass with more Jack Daniel's, drew a long slurp, and went to the bathroom to take a leak. From there he spoke loudly for Isaac's benefit. "Look, I never told you this before, because I knew you didn't want to hear it, but you seem to be in a better mood at the moment. So listen; I never liked that place; I always hated that place, always knew that some kind of bad shit was going to go down there one of those days. When you didn't call that morning, hell, I knew, I knew all right. Why else would I go all the way up there and hound the sheriff? Took him two hours to get off his ass, but he finally did it. I shook him up, we kept calling and calling, but he knew you were nuts, he'd read your shit, and we boogied down those back roads and we found you all. Oh yes, how we found you."

He finished and moved back into the living room, to the couch, and saw that Isaac no longer sat there. Instead, the ghost of his friend had sneaked past him and now admired the bookshelves, glancing at titles.

"Is there any way I can talk you out of that so you're sorta paying attention to me, Isaac? See, uh, yeah, I'm far too drunk to actually confirm that you're here, I mean here, right in front of me, uh, yeah, not only in my drunken mind but in my house. So if you've got to do that whole spectral gig, I'd rather you stayed in one place and just did, like, magical shit around you. You could, you know, levitate my stuff if you felt inclined, and so forth."

Isaac Maelstrom returned to the couch.

"You're not talking tonight. You never talked much, but what's this silent treatment? God, I wish Lisa were here to tell me I'm not crazy."

*Beautiful girl,* Isaac seemed to say, with something very ugly playing there in his wispy nonvoice.

"What the fuck you say it like that for? Yeah, she is. So I've only known her a short time, but she's the best thing that's ever happened to me, I think. What, you don't believe me, you think I'm shitting you? What, you mad that I'm not up at your place, watching over your son? You think I'm scared, right? Well, I am, I have been, I am now! Hey, hey, none of this shit is my fault, right, all right? What, you're *judging* me?"

With a burst of courage and equilibrium that he didn't think he possessed, Wakely sidestepped an end table and threw himself at the dead man on the couch. "You always knew that you scared me, didn't you, Isaac?"

*Yes.*

"Of course you did. Even when we were only going through the galleys or playing with bids from the houses, or just downing a couple of beers watching a ball game trying to pretend we were being the way the normal folks are, trying to make like everything was all right, you frightened me."

Wakely finished off the JD and dropped the glass on the floor; he had perhaps four or five minutes' worth of consciousness left before this agonizing night finally pulled the plug on him. He knelt on the couch and tried to keep balanced, sort of sitting up the way a dog will, getting closer to the dead. "Tell me, pal, my old pal, my good and trusted friend . . . why? Why'd it happen like that? Why'd your daughter kill you, why leave Jacob alive? Why did she kill herself? What did you do to her?"

*Nothing,* Isaac said.

"Oh, oh, that's rich."

*He made her do it.*

"Jacob?"

*Because of me. I imprisoned him on the island because of it.*

"Because of what?"

*Because I stole it all from him, all that talent; none of it belonged to me.*

Wakely shuddered, maybe catching some of what it meant but probably not. He said, "I always figured that kid murdered you all." His eyes unfocused past the point of no return, his head angled sideways as the muscles in his lower lip collapsed. Looking like a hydrocephalic child, his head too heavy to carry anymore, he slumped forward and gurgled. He still had a fragmented thought or two in his mind, but didn't care much at this point if he were lying across the lap of a long-decayed friend—and watched from somewhere close by, and yet outside of himself, how Isaac Maelstrom, perhaps insane even in death, began to weep.

*And now I'm the one who's too frightened to go home.*

# *Chapter Twenty-two*

Her fingers still tingled from where she'd touched his forehead and could feel all the disfigured things that slithered and cowered in there.

Fighting back a swell of revulsion, Katie moved aside and began to wash Lisa's black eyes, trying desperately not to fade back into that comforting oblivion she'd known in the hospital and Nana's bedroom. Something pulled at her, nice and cool and soothing, but she resisted the draw.

People stood nearby. Voices she recognized, but somehow couldn't quite distinguish, chattered and conferred at length. Tim and the baby, she thought, and Grandpa, Olivetti, the woman with the rosaries who didn't just pray now, but actually spoke in conversation, Nana slurping coffee, all of them talking as if at a party. She heard a clatter of plates and glasses, chairs pushed back, and a lot of laughter, as if they had just finished dinner without her. She shut her eyes, hoping to hear herself at the gathering, and tried to listen to exactly what she had to say for herself.

"What?" Jacob asked.

Katie looked over at him leaning against the wall and staring out his bedroom window. "Excuse me?" She sounded weak, but shrill.

"I thought you said something."

"No," she told him, but maybe she had. She couldn't quite distinguish what she was doing anymore, or what she should be doing instead of simply waiting. Lisa's lips moved in her sleep, her eyes occasionally fluttering open, then easing shut again. "Will the morning help us?"

He looked puzzled, and then he understood. "Like in my books, you mean?" He grinned sadly, and some innocence remained in his face. "Sunrise scaring off the devil, something like that?" He shrugged.

*Talk about avoiding issues.* They needed to figure this out, and he proved worse at broaching the subject than she did. Perhaps he truly was suicidal, the last decade nothing more than one long arc of flight from a cliff, the whole time just waiting to hit bottom.

Katie took a shot and hoped she could word it correctly. "Is this all because of you?"

He knew what she meant. The mark, the bloody mark, all these stains. He and Katie were moving closer together even in the silence. She began to understand and believe. "I'd kill myself if it would help, but it wouldn't. It would only make them stronger. I might even wind up with them."

"Yes, I think you're right." She trusted him implicitly at this point, having felt the honesty of his madness when they'd made their contact. She believed him, whatever he said, even about the bridge being destroyed, and that they were trapped. Katie knew it had to be true, because anything insane was truth with him.

Lisa had no broken bones, though she

probably did have a hairline fracture in her left arm and some bruised vertebrae. She wasn't hemorrhaging, and Katie hoped everything with the baby would be fine. Lisa had always been much stronger than she was, and so couldn't be confined to the same emotional or physical limits as Katie put on herself; Lisa wasn't delirious or having an avoidance reaction—she continued to grow more alert, and didn't simply want to sleep and forget what had transpired.

"Why an ax?" Katie asked.

"I don't know," Jacob said. He sounded like a little boy who couldn't beg test answers off of anybody.

"It's such a clumsy way to try to kill someone. I can't stop thinking about it. You raise it high into the air, both your arms overhead, and by the time you swing down to chop off somebody's head, the person has plenty of time to run. It doesn't make any sense."

"Rachel won't tell me what happened," he said. "None of them will."

"Where's your father?"

"He's hiding. Cowering."

"What does that mean?"

He scowled out the window, his head tilted as if listening to a good song on a Walkman.

Katie felt the incredible urge to keep after

it, though she understood he'd said all he could. "Wouldn't they hate her? Wouldn't your brother despise her? Crazy as it was, I saw them there for a moment standing over Lise, and they looked like they were in love."

With a groan, Lisa opened her eyes and kept them open, squinting Eastwood-style. She gave the room a slow once-over, and Katie could feel the all-inclusive hate seeping from her friend.

"Relax," Katie said.

"We're still here?" Her voice sounded thick and dry with blood and dust. "Why the fuck are we still here?"

"We're in Jacob's bedroom. It's okay."

"Oh, that's precious," Lisa said. It came out as little more than a croak, puffed lips giving her a lisp. "Relax, yeah, really. Why aren't we wheeling out of here at a hundred and ten miles an hour? Where are the cops?"

"You remember what happened?"

"Of course I fucking remember what happened. Do you know what happened? Where are those two lunatics? Why are we here?"

"The bridge is out."

"Out?" Lisa threw on a smile, and it was the ugliest thing that Katie had ever seen in her life. Lisa hacked a humorless guffaw, followed by a heinous titter. "What does that mean, it's out? How is it out?" Her gaze searched the room and locked onto Jacob by the window. "What? A well-placed tree blocking the way? You did it, didn't you? You and your friends."

"I'm sorry, Lisa," he said.

"You piece of shit bastard." Lisa slowly ran her hands over her stomach, inspecting the cuts. She didn't act as if she were trying to feel the baby within, or appear to wonder if it was gone. She sat up and swung an arm out, shoving Katie aside, and slowly, groaning but almost grinning, all the red hair framing her face, like a caricature of his sister, she sneered nearly as well as Rachel did. "I'm going to kill them. Where are they?"

He simply looked at her.

Katie tried to say something, but nothing came.

"They weren't crazy fans," Lisa hissed. "They had your eyes. Who are they, Jacob? Where are they now?"

He couldn't imagine.

Katie felt for Lisa's hand and had to fight to grip it when Lisa struggled, trying to pull away. She wondered why she was being as rational as she was; it didn't feel right to act this way. Katie felt as if there was a cloud of stupor hiding around the next emotional corner, just waiting to leap out and smother her in its tender, suffocating clench. Her cheeks grew hot, her chest aching with something trying to get out. Lisa kept tugging her fist away, but Katie held on tightly with both hands, for her own sake. She squirmed closer and made an effort to hug her, careful of all the bruises and scrapes, trembling now, Lisa's swollen lips doing their best to flatten into a bloodless line of indifference.

"You're fiction," Katie moaned to him.

"No, I'm not," he said, but feared that she told the truth. "I need your help."

So he told them everything.

His life didn't take long to spill, and neither did his death. He ran it out as quickly and candidly as possible, not even pausing to check whether they believed him or not, or if Lisa was getting ready to crush his skull with the lamp. When he mentioned the muses they heard him in the forest, and one of them skittered across the roof and down through the trees. Katie kept managing to take it all in without shutting down. Lisa, perhaps willing to believe in the living dead after attempted rape, nodded sagely, understanding why so much evil had flowed across her tonight. She'd been lost in the madhouse and now realized how and why she'd been captured by the mansion. He kept talking, laying it all out on the line, incapable of sounding ashamed anymore. The storm grew worse. Distant howls and yips erupted from time to time, so human in their need. The deceased continued to crawl in and out of the maelstrom.

"With cruelty," Lisa said. "With blood on their tongues."

"So I'm sane?" Katie said, unsure if that were even possible at this point. "Relatively so, that's all I mean."

"Yes, of course."

"As in, say, compared to the guy in the Macy's parking lot licking the grille of a Buick, shouting, 'Waffles, waffles'? At least as sane as that?"

*Comedy,* Dad had said. *Use humor and build on it at random, since that's the way the process works. The horror gimmick won't be complete without a few laughs thrown in to underscore the fear.*

"It was never a gimmick," Jacob said.

The sentence was not meant to be said out loud.

*Words fail.*

Katie couldn't take her eyes off his lips. "What happened?" she asked. "What came next?"

"I don't remember."

"Try."

"I can't."

"You have to."

"Tell us," Lisa said. "Tell yourself."

*Sentences. Men fail.*

Katie tugged on his arm and saw just then, like watching an ill reflection of herself exploding from the darkness, what was suddenly behind him, coming out from the closet: a sickly younger woman, who reached out with both arms, waves of ink lapping around her, to seize and pull him in.

"Jacob, my love," Elizabeth said. "It's time."

"No!" Katie screamed, knowing how insane the girl was, and so understanding how big a truth she played in his life.

Jacob fell into the closet, where he had perhaps really died, and vanished.

# *Chapter Twenty-three*

Ophelia swam.

Coursing through the pond and careful not to brush against any dense weeds or rotting branches sticking up from the shallows, she looped and fell into a languid repose. On her back, beneath the moon once more after so long, breathing in the world again. She shook her hair out, dove, driving herself powerfully down and across to the opposite shore.

She stood and stepped into the thick grass,

so many shadows moving in the woods, shifting positions as she came near and walked among them. So much fear. For all of the dread, these circles and meetings scarcely meant anything. The muses had run, spoken, and made their love with one another, and would continue to do so. The men's beards grew long and tangled, their hands scarred from fighting—the women's lips and smooth skin were left less soft by their desire, rolled against the rocks.

"Do you dream?" she asked.

She did not know them much anymore. She believed they must, and that she must, though she couldn't remember. She combed through their matted hair, her fingernails grazing muscular chest and shoulders, lightly kissing those who wept. Muses placed their ears to her belly and listened to the child waft and murmur. They could all hear a difference in the songs of the dark tonight. In the pulse of the rain.

A symphony built in blood and love, a capella redemption or damnation.

Where did they belong in the maelstrom?

Ophelia was of them all, understanding their desire, and the want of the dead. Regarding that lady, her name was Thrush. She was the lovely one atop the spruce, sitting with her knees bent looking up at treetops, slowly spreading and refolding her wings, a charmer of winds moving her mouth to sonnets. How many angles of her nose and cheekbones could be ascribed to Rachel? The length of her eyelashes was from Joseph. There, crawling from the roots, came possum, whom Rachel had always been particularly fond of. Eyes empty, flat, and black as shale.

Ophelia didn't dance, but swooned and let each of them run their hands over her belly. The rain splashed against skin and scale and fur.

Katie didn't have time to think about what she was doing as she dove toward the closet after Jacob, the slamming door catching her high and hard in the shoulder, slapping her away. She flew backward with a grunt, hit the footboard of the bed, and slid to the floor.

A strange sound eased out of Lisa's throat, like venom sacs filling. "This is some party," she said.

"That little bitch," Katie hissed at the departed sickly dead girl. So much of Katie resided in that face, the same kind of loss and strain, and willingness to burden others with her own grief. She scrambled forward, grabbed the knob, and kicked at the door, banging on it.

"You hear them?" Lisa asked.

"No."

"They're gone. You just lost your thesis."

Suddenly Katie felt a wave of remorse and guilt, for having set them on this course tonight, following down a track that had been laid for her years ago, and doing nothing at any point to get off. "I'm sorry, Lise." Not only hadn't she tried hard enough to get off this road, but she'd ushered her best friend onto it as well.

"I know. I am, too. It's not your fault."

Ghosts had been with them for a long time—if you've been haunted by one you've known them all. Tim was still here in the room, the dust falling like cocaine. She looked at the bruises and scratches, the welts and bite marks, and knew the maelstrom had done it to her. "I'm so sorry."

"So am I. Really, I am. You can't love him, Katie. You can't."

"No, you're right, it's impossible."

"In this house anything is possible, but that doesn't matter now. We need to get the fuck out of here."

In the hallway, the wheelchair butted the bedroom door.

## The Deceased

Summer solstice, the high holy sabbath of witches, and Beth watching him. Scarecrow hay, in the fields, the dead. And honey.

Wearing her yellow dress, with her chestnut hair drawn slightly to one side and affixed with a red bow, looking even more beautiful than before, if possible: not so frail, but her face still much too pale, the startling whiteness accentuating the dark circles under her eyes.

So he simply stared at her now, in the shadows of his mind, her aura of love, loyalty, and dedication so powerful that he couldn't find the door out of here anymore. Sorrow creased the edges of her cheeks and he moved closer to her—but not too close, not sure of where exactly they were, or ever had been, or how far away she remained. Distances became irrelevant on Stonethrow, especially in the bowels of the house. He moved, perhaps against the wall of the closet, perhaps only farther inside himself, but soon he felt Beth holding him.

"You don't want to be here," she said, wielding the accusation well, slashing deeply with just the right inflection.

"I'm here."

"You said you would come back to me."

"And I have."

"No, no, you haven't. You won't." She shook her head, the bow wagging back and forth. "But I'll help you. I'll lead you."

That sounded as much a blessing as a threat.

A pregnant pause then, the silence as heavy as Ophelia's womb; he stood waiting for death to puff against his face and whistle down across his chafed wrists. "All right, Beth."

She looked at him with a frown of resignation, as if she didn't want to follow through on what she must now do, but would do it anyway. "Come with me and I'll show you, the way you once showed me." She took his hand, and he wondered if at last he'd find the answer to exactly who she was, and why she'd always been here with him.

Jacob followed into the night of his shattered soul.

He saw himself.

# Chapter Twenty-four

*What did she do with their heads?*

Jacob and Elizabeth watched as Jacob watches Rachel and Joseph—with most of their clothes on—making love to a woman in an open area of dry leaves. His brother sees him glaring from behind the bushes and motions him over. Rachel laughs huskily among a staccato of dry sobs, and the performance is outlandish but nothing he is not already accustomed to by now. Still, he doesn't want to witness any more. Rachel snaps branches in her fists, her teeth coming together on her tongue. With a hissing moan his brother falls lazily on the dark-skinned woman, this new lady love.

The three of them lie in the leaves exhausted. Their backs are muddy, their breath causing a stir in the sand. His sister's nose runs and her cheeks are red, her lips with a little blood on them. She likes to nip. She stares at Jacob with a hungry but sexless smile that both frightens and tempts him with awful fuel. She urges him to give in, to join in, to get in, and to give up.

A man saunters forward from the other side of the clearing, grinning childishly, heading for Rachel. Jacob guns a look at the stranger, and the man's feet shift as the soil beneath him steams and cracks. It's raccoon, with his arched eyebrows and ugly ears, his bottom lip that hangs in a black vee. He grabs his shaggy head with unclipped fingernails, yelps, and drops to the ground. Convulsing, the man whines and slowly manages to crawl away.

This is instinct unloosed. Rachel sees the need in all of them, and uses it in whatever way she sees fit. She crooks a finger at Jacob, ordering him without useless words, commanding with motions and position. An incredible calm passes into her face, something Jacob has never seen there before: a genuine love for him.

He runs.

He passes his own muses layered all over the forest like a carpet of delinquents, wallowing in depravity, wondering where it is they go so that his parents never find them. Or do they? Raccoon is slumped against a log, and the man grunts sadly. "She wanted me."

"She wants us all."

Eventually Jacob reels to the house, where construction on a new series of rooms has been completed only a month ago. Rooms he doesn't intend to go into, that no one will probably ever need to enter. They're coupled like barnacles onto the corner of the west wing, and he sees that the shutters haven't been secured, and are clapping freely in the rising wind.

He rests his head against the front door and enters quietly, the pounding in his side easing as he crosses the hallway. Mom is vacuuming the living-room carpet, singing off-key loudly to herself. Above the roar he can still hear the echoes of his father's typewriter clacking along the corridors.

There are traps here.

His mother must know the truth: she and Dad are only performing a complicated play, acting so oblivious. Isolation is lonely murder. Soon she will begin ripping out her flowers, sowing the ground with gravel. What the hell can they possibly think his brother and sister do out there in the woods all day long? What reason does Mother come up with when she sees them exhausted and smiling, returning to the house disheveled and dirty? Her children crawl in the mud. Can't she see the difference that has come over them? Or has she known from the start that in the maelstrom there are no surprises, only static madness?

Where is Dad?

"Hey, sport," Mom says as the grating sound of the vacuum dies off. She checks the filter bag, glances at his face, then his feet, and asks, "What's the matter?"

"Nothing." He adds to the lie that has become their repetitive scene, because he has joined as part of their play.

"No, honey?"

"No."

"You sure?"

"Yes," he hisses, letting it drag out in anxiety for too long. "I'm sure."

"You just kicked out the vacuum plug and

didn't even notice. . . . You're dragging your feet and wearing a frown that drops lower than your knees. So, come on, spill it, what's the problem?"

He stares into her eyes and she says nothing more. They regard one another emptily and he slowly comes to the realization that his mother is a cardboard cutout, two-dimensional and being worked like a paper doll. There is no depth, no reality to her existence. Even now, when she sounds aggressive, almost powerful, it serves no purpose.

Floating on a tide of ink in the closet, Jacob and Elizabeth heard Dad's typewriter, and he noticed now what he didn't see then—how his mother's bottom lip quivers, as if she might break into sobs, or dissolve layer by layer. Perhaps they could have escaped together, if only he'd had more faith in her validity.

"Plug in the vacuum, please," Mom says, and Jacob does. The machine drones on. He heads upstairs, about to go to his room and contemplate his own retreat, when he decides he must make an effort to speak to his father.

His hand slides along the banister as he moves to Dad's study in the attic. The aroma of old books fills the hallway, the taste of paper thick in the air. A spark in the room would start a conflagration that would probably burn for two days straight. The door is slightly ajar, and the familiar clacking sounds like nothing other than slaps across well-muscled flesh. Instead of music this is a boxing match. His father fights, and has always fought.

"Beth . . ." Jacob said, watching himself about to learn how to hate the man, a rancor he still felt.

"Shhhh."

"Dad . . . ?" Jacob says.

"I'm a little busy now, son."

Of course he is; he always is, busy dealing with whatever drives against the inside of his skull, seeking exit. Dad is busy opening doors. "But I'd like to—"

"Yes, okay, Jacob, in a little while."

His breathing hitches until he's almost gasping, the sight of Rachel turning over her love to him consuming him for an instant. There's more of a command in his voice now, like talking to a muse. "Listen to me—"

"Not now," his father says, his gaze supplanted to the paper, his fingers flying over the keys, fast, so breakneck.

"But, Dad? I—"

"Later." His father sits bent in his seat, bulging shoulder blades rising like furled wings on his back. How it must hurt when he finally lies back to rest, bones creaking and popping in place.

Jacob stands in the doorway to his father's soul, lost, wavering between taking another step into the room and backing out slowly with his black thoughts. He looks around, taking in the plaques and honorary degrees, the annotated set of Poe's works, other science fiction, fantasy and horror novels thrown without care on the tables and lying open on the floor, thousands of manuscript pages stacked on low shelves in the corner. Once they found a family of rats living in a nest made from his father's *Strange Water Tales*. Dad cared for them and eventually set them free in the back fields. All around Jacob remain odd mementos from his Dad's own childhood, and relics of his grandfather, Taddy's mariner's sextant and spyglass, and so on through Maelstrom history.

He tries once more, his voice breaking with the full extent of his fear and pain, which suddenly strikes without warning.

"Daddy . . . ?" He moans.

"Get out! Get out of here, you!" his father growls, swinging in his seat, his index finger jabbing the air violently on the word *you*, at his son, making it completely clear that the only one who must get out—who must ever leave here—is Jacob.

Beth scratched at his neck lightly.

Dad turns back to his typewriter and begins the ferocious dance again.

Jacob gets out, not quite as afraid, angry, or disappointed as he would have thought. Somehow, among all these motions and events, he has come to conclusions that prove something, and yet prove nothing. He trembles, feeling his brother and sister in the forest, aware of them always. The edges of his vision glow and continue to brighten, knives prodding from within his skull. The vacuum roars as if sucking up torsos and animal tusks.

He barely gets to his room before a wave of nausea sends him shivering to his knees. Dry heaves leave him helpless for minutes before he has the strength to clamber onto the bed. Tears dribble onto his pillows, and he chews the blankets. This is the worst it's been for weeks, and no one is near to help him through it. He is alone—that's the price of getting out, for now and forever alone—and his fingernails begin to shred the feathery contents of his pillow.

Empathizing with his former self, feeling it all over again inside his own head, Jacob held his hands to his temples, as it happened to him once more, even in here, where nothing else existed.

The noise of the typing grows louder, Dad rallying in his fight, taking control of the waltz.

Jacob rolls over onto his back and tastes blood, feeling so much of himself abruptly shear off—but not the agony—as the closet door slowly swings open. There is sudden color: a world of yellow with a splash of red.

A girl stands there in that place where he hangs his winter clothes and stores his board games. Yet she doesn't appear to be lacking for space. The smell of honey wafts off her chestnut hair, and an appealing smile eases the horrors looming inside his head. She bobs her chin at him as a sign of mixed greeting and curiosity, as if she'd just turned around and found him there staring into her bedroom. Her yellow dress is from another time, something that Taddy's daughters might have worn—Jacob has seen the photographs. Perhaps a new curtain has been drawn back. The red bow in her hair almost comically pulls a few brown curls to one side, as he stares into the closet and smiles at her, regarding the grin easing wider on her face, and also sees there behind her into a place that shouldn't have such depth, so far back in an abruptly looming haze of mired years of murder to come, inside the closet stands—

"Jesus Christ," Jacob said. "He can see me."

"Hi," the girl says.

"Hello." He has no reason to do anything besides be polite.

"What's your name?"

"You know my name," he whispers, rising from the bed. The headache is gone, despite the clattering of his father above, who is throwing books around because he's hit a block. The typewriter's silence is all at once the most beautiful song he's ever heard played; at last he can think.

"Yes, you're Jacob. Do you know my name?"

He thinks he does, or should, but nothing comes to him. A few moments ago perhaps he would have known, but not anymore. "No."

"I'm Elizabeth."

That sounds right, and he nods. "Yes, of course. I know that. It's a nice name, Elizabeth."

"Thank you. I like yours, too."

"Do you?"

"Yes."

"What are you doing in there?"

"Nothing."

He chuckles because this is never the truth; there is always something happening in this house. "What would you like to do?"

"Let's play checkers."

"Sure, okay." She can't be one of Taddy's daughters if she knows about checkers, though she might have learned by wading through his games. He reaches beyond her into the closet, searching and finding nothing to the touch, and yet when he withdraws his hands he is somehow holding the taped-up box with the checkerboard in it.

"I want to be red," Elizabeth says.

"Sure."

In the back of the closet, Beth put her hands to his face and pulled him roughly to one side, forcing him to stare directly into her eyes with those black trenches dug below them. "You were my only friend," he mumbled to her, touching the creases above her brow. "Why are you sick now after all this time . . . ?"

She kissed him deeply while he plays checkers with the dead a decade ago, half the board in the closet, half sticking out into the room. "This night of your reign is almost over, darling," Beth said, and Beth says, "King me."

267

# Chapter Twenty-five

Joseph in the wheelchair, or perhaps only the wheelchair, tried to get through.

Whispered laughter, somewhat soothing music, and the beating thunder rattling the windows made Katie wheel and spin again, facing the door, then the closet, now staring outside. Lisa chuckled to herself, getting a little out of this.

She said, "Joey, my boy, you ready to play again?"

The door shuddered in its frame.

"Think we can get out by the window?" Katie asked.

"No, but even if we could what difference would it make? We'd be outside in the storm. They'd only catch us there. We're already *caught*. They just like to take their time."

Lightning showered the room with brilliance, revealing just how haggard they looked.

"The only way out is through the closet," Katie said. So strange to say it, but so befitting here in the house.

Lisa was squinting, her lips set into a humorous sneer, her fiery bangs stuck to the sweat and crusting blood on her forehead. "He's dead already, or joined up with his family. Your hallowed literary heroic figure is a crock. He's no romantic leading man either, Kathleen; he isn't coming back for us."

"He will if he can."

"Bullshit. You saw her. He's found his love, and she's murdered. He probably killed her a long time ago."

"No."

"Yes, fuck that shit. Like hell, no."

"Like hell, yes," said Jacob's mother, the lady with the melting face, with hardly enough of a mouth to speak with. She stepped free from the shadows as if having always been a part of them, oozing strand by strand to form this incomplete creature. "You'll have to hurry if you want to get out. My children are crazy, but Isaac is almost here, and that will be worse than you can possibly imagine."

Katie could imagine a lot.

Even before she remembered she had a history of insanity and murder, she knew there were other matters to consider.

When she was thirteen she dreamed she had been walking home from middle school when Jeff Rimmer, a boy in her science class she liked a lot, and punched and pinched most of the time because of it—he pinched her back once and she stabbed him in the finger with a pencil. His mother called her mother to complain and Daddy yelled because it had been a stupid and dangerous thing to do, and he'd have to pay the doctor's bill—all right, maybe she was shutting down now, not wanting to think about anything anymore, though the memories surged as the woman stared at her. But in the dream, Jeffrey Rimmer had jumped out from behind a high wall of untrimmed hedges and threw a bucket of burning coals in her face, shouting in a voice that wasn't his, "The oven is warming."

Her mind remained dented with the nightmare for a few days more, but it had mostly been pounded out after another week. It made her vomit one morning but meant nothing much until the afternoon of a science test. Jeffrey had been absent from school for three days and was about to ruin his already borderline grades. Somebody mentioned his name. And somebody else, and still others. By lunch the background buzzing of other students grew so loud and abstract that she had to tug hard on the sweatshirt of smelly Harold Palazzo, Jeffrey's best friend, and ask him what was going on.

It happened like this, Katie remembered, while Jacob's mother, with just enough muscle left in her eyebrow to cock it, gave her a frown. Harold turned around in his seat and stared with such a tangible and scathing malice that she thought he was going to smash her teeth out. "Don't you know anything?" he asked, a question with no response possible other than putting her fists on her hips and giving a dumbfounded smirk, which she admitted wasn't much of a reply at all. No, she didn't know anything. She grabbed him harder, feeling the fear taking out large chunks of

her stomach, and Harold flung her back in
her chair with one hard shove, shouting so
loudly that the lunch monitors rushed over to
pull him away before he got the chance to
really hurt her. He had a rolling eye that
seemed to contemplate perdition. "He's
dead," Harold hissed, and then Katie realized, oh, oh, yes, she did know something,
and she knew it for no reason at all. "Their
house burned down. It's been on the news, in
the papers; the principal made an announce-
ment three days ago." Shouting kids sum-
moned two teachers to help keep Harold
from wringing Katie's neck. "There was a
mass and everyone from town showed up;
your parents were there, how could you not
know?" Even as the teachers lifted him up
and drew Harold from the room he savagely
held on to the table and struggled to get at
her. He was finally hauled away, but she
could still hear him shrieking from down the
corridors, "How could you not know!"

Katie didn't know how she couldn't have
known, except, of course, that she had. After
the day at Nana's, though, she suspected anything of herself, realizing exactly what it was
that flowed in the blood. Perhaps she'd
burned down Jeffrey's house, angry because
he hadn't asked her to the movies. For years

afterward she didn't think of that dream again, or Jeffrey Rimmer, until reading *Fadeaway* brought it all back to her in one swift and almost loving chop to the throat—a chapter where a kid leaves school early and goes home and puts his head in an oven, not realizing you can't gas yourself that way anymore, but frying your face is another matter, and the house burns down, killing the rest of his family as well.

Christ, the cocaine already had her wired to the max by then, jittery while waiting for Tim to get home for the night, and the supernatural thriller only added to the tension, the waxlike ball of memory that suddenly started dribbling over her again. It had not only added to her irrational thoughts but fired them, pumped them, greased them up. To write like that, inject and infect, to absorb her nightmare and return it to her. She flipped the book over in her hands to look for a backjacket photograph of the author, and found none.

But soon, in studying him, she learned more about dead families, and understood their connection in blood.

The wheelchair scratched at the door.

Katie flung herself forward, no longer so afraid of Jacob's mother, who quickly unwound into the shadows, pulling her own fadeaway, with her nose pointing over toward the closet.

"Wait, help us . . . !"

Another chuckle from Lisa, who realized no one else, especially a woman who'd been decapitated ten years ago, could help them now. "Come on in, Joey," she said loudly enough to be heard in the hallway. "You're stuck here for a reason, aren't you? In the house and out in the forest, you dirty little boy. You like roughing up the girls, playing with the kids. Hey, Joey, you sure your dad didn't lock you away on this island for a reason, like maybe he knew you were the kind of fucking nutcase who hangs around pre-schools? Did you turn your piece of shit sister, too? Was she just budding her titties when you got your hands in her pants when she was sleeping on the couch? What'd you do to your baby brother, Joey? What'd you and your sister do to him out there in the dirt?"

She knew they were out there, straining for flesh.

Katie shouted to them. "He's finally caught up with you. He'll be joining you two soon, fuckers."

But no, not true, he hadn't caught up with

them; the sick woman had dragged him away from this fight, down into another one.

*I can do this; I can help him.* She took the doorknob to the closet firmly in her fist and opened it easily. The interior loomed wider than possible, a deeper darkness in the shadows hiding there. All the dark pages she'd read from them were a part of it, from out of their lives and into their deaths. She spun back to watch Lisa pounding on the bedroom door, as if she really wanted out of here, to get her hands on his brother and sister again and make them bleed much worse than she had. Katie took a step. It was easy, like getting up off the brick stoop and walking into the house to see what could be seen. Something filled her hand, and the dead woman whispered in her ear. She tightened her fist, felt a smooth affirmation of substance, but saw nothing there yet. Whispering continued and she said, "Yeah?" She moved closer, still in the room, but now no longer a part of it, hoping against hope—as all her hopes were hoped against—that in this separate place she would find Jacob, and not Grandpa or Tim or the baby.

The door slammed shut behind her.

*       *       *

Doubling over in agony, Ophelia reached out for support from Rabbit and Worm and the other muses surrounding her, helping her over to the thickly matted bed of grass at the edge of the woods. Labor pains came more quickly now, like a bear trap opening and abruptly snapping shut again within her. The child knew its father had returned, waiting to be born under his eye. She fought against the pain until her knees buckled and she could no longer stand.

Worm worked his hand into Ophelia's mouth, and she bit down, tasting his loving blood as the joy of this event overshadowed all anguish. Her legs gave out just as Deer laid her beside the pond, spreading her legs further and letting her feet rest in the comforting water. Her green and white hair trailed across the dappled surface, rain churning up the green froth.

She gasped and the muses nodded, understanding that at long last it was time, each of them frightened but intrigued at what the new birth might mean for them. Veins like serpents writhed in Ophelia's throat, yellow eyes igniting as she panted for breath. The child, the child. Staring back toward the house she whimpered. "My Liege, my Lucifer . . ."

The woods wept.

The child pushed to be free, waiting no longer.

# *Chapter Twenty-six*

Jacob made eye contact with himself as a boy and whispered, "This isn't a dream."

The kid cocks his head and says back, "This isn't real."

Mom enters the room and announces supper is ready, and instantly Elizabeth vanishes, the checkers scattered as if from a breeze. His mother wanders over, puzzled, making a face that's at least half a frown, and asks, "What were you looking for in there?" He shrugs, and that seems to placate her. She is easily dismissed, Mother is, because she so seldom wants to be doing whatever she does. Mom is more sullen lately, Dad hardly ever talking, the clacking growing louder as if he's hung his head on the dash bar. Now it starts again. A shard of summer sunlight slashes through the window and lands firmly across Jacob's eyes, blinding him.

Jacob reared more deeply into the closet, thinking that the ax was coming soon, soon; he could feel it.

Out of the stirred and flowing darkness of ink he heard footsteps far behind. Beth seemed more frightened now, her fingers drawing against his face as if she tried to carve somebody else's likeness from his skin. He touched her dress, and that proved to be as good as any other time he'd ever touched a woman.

"What did I promise you, Beth?"

His voice is as empty of life as that of any other Maelstrom in the house. He remembers Dad crying, pulling him by the throat. The ax.

"You promised me blood," Elizabeth said.

He bleeds from a paper cut he's just received from a five-hundred-dollar bill, and sucks on the side of his finger, unaware that his mother is standing in the doorway behind him with a basketful of clean laundry. She shakes her head resolutely, about to yell. She gets like this sometimes, when the world is too large for her to handle alone. She drops the basket and flees down the hall, shouting up to the attic. "Isaac! Come down here to Jacob's room immediately!"

The call resonates across the house, the fields, and the forest. The call will settle everything in a few moments. Startled, Jacob drops the dice and scatters the hotels Elizabeth has on New York and New Jersey, the three houses on the red Monopoly. His mother is furious, and he knows he's in trouble, caught; he's been nailed—but the closet is only partway open, and from mother's angle she can't see in.

His fear abates. "Hi, Mom," he says, expecting no answer. He receives none. She picks up the basket again and holds it before her like a shield or a weapon. She looks down at him over the pile of clothes as though disappointed or insulted, a woman who's discovered that a diamond is actually only cut glass. He turns back and stares into the closet and sees Elizabeth replacing the house on the red border of Kentucky. Why is she here?

281

And far behind her, why are they still staring at him from within the dark?

The call is bringing his father.

"What are you doing?" Mom asks.

"Nothin'."

"Nothing, huh?"

"No."

"Just playing Monopoly in your closet by yourself."

"Just playin'."

His mother empties his clothes onto his bed and begins folding them, putting them away in the bureau. She mutters to herself, neither winning nor losing her own argument. She sets aside what goes in the closet, waiting for his father to arrive before breaching that stronghold. Her movements are mechanical; slow and indecisive, as if she must think about how to place her hands, force her blood through her own veins. "Are you that lonely? Can you really be that mad at the rest of us?"

"I'm not mad." He licks at the thin line of blood welling again from the paper cut.

She slaps his shirts and socks into his drawers. "You won't talk to us, you don't go outside much even though it's so lovely on the island. Rachel says you've never taken the time to go and see the caves and orchards.

You talk to your father only when you're asking questions about writing, and you don't help around the house much anymore . . . so tell me what's wrong."

Such a catalog of petty slights. He wonders how many he could list, and if it would ever end. "Nothin'."

"Stop dropping the *g*'s off your-*ing* endings. You're doing it more and more lately."

"Sorry."

"Don't be sorry. Just try to stop it."

He rolls the dice and moves his race car down the board. "Sorry."

The face Mom makes is caught squarely between a snarl and a leer. She does that a lot, creates a new emotion to exemplify what he's putting her through. "I said don't be sorry."

The squeak of Joseph's wheelchair echoes in the hall. Rachel pushes him along the ramps, and within the space of a few of Beth's calm breaths they're in his room now, too—his brother and sister smiling and showing off their perfect teeth, their wonderfully licked lips.

Look at the three of them now, everybody positioned as if to ensnare him inside. Beth remains seated in the closet, reading the back of the cards because she's still confused over how to mortgage her property. Jacob spins and stands, hardly any taller than his brother in the chair.

That ego and self-contained confidence of Joseph's never wavers for a moment. "What are you hiding in your closet, Third? Some dirty magazines?"

It's an ambush.

Jacob lifts his stare to his sister. She braces her foot on the carpet and veers off from pushing any further into the room. Joseph frowns but says nothing, doesn't even try to roll his own wheels. They've become a unit, and so often she is in control.

Dad is coming closer.

His family sets upon him, and behind him, he feels Elizabeth's urging. In the deep darkness he notices himself again, and what is to become of them all. The man doesn't try to talk him out of anything.

Elizabeth is dead, and she hissed at him, licking his ear as he regarded himself as a boy and saw the building pressure in the kid's evil eyes. "I love you," Beth told him. "Your family didn't. No one ever did or ever will, not even that stupid insane woman who thinks she can save you. Only me."

Dad walks in.

There's no air of dignity to him, no power; nothing to satisfy, respect, or even fear de-

spite the pain. This is his father, who seems
to know what is about to happen, as if he has
lived and died through it many times before.
"What's wrong?" he says, already knowing
the answers.

"Look here," Mom tells him, pointing at the
visible corner of the Monopoly board. "Our
son has an imaginary friend."

Dad's smile is composed of plastic, not
flesh. "So?"

"So. Is that all you're going to say? So."

"What's the problem with that?"

Rachel, standing behind the wheelchair,
leans forward. Her hands do a slow slide
down Joseph's shoulders, to his chest, and for
a barely distinguished instant she tweaks at
his nipples. She wants to see just how far she
can push it in front of their parents. The tip
of her tongue juts from the corner of her
mouth.

Drawing her chin back, her hands on her
hips, Mother rolls her eyes. "You were the one
who only a week ago said—"

"I know what I said."

". . . that we've been lax in our tutoring and
that the Board of National Education is going
to administer tests soon, and now that he's
taken to emulating you as a writer there's a
greater chance—"

"Please," Jacob and Dad say as one, and then, startled, look at each another.

". . . that this . . . exile . . . or whatever you want to call it, may be harming him. Christ, sometimes I hear him talking all night long."

"I'm sorry," Jacob says.

"Stop being sorry!" she shouts, then turns to his father again. "I told you we needed to get out of here; we've all been suffering from isolation out here and becoming more and more taciturn. We need to get back to the city for a while. Don't you think so? Don't you? Now?"

Nodding, as if in complete agreement, Dad bellows, "No, I don't!" Joseph grips the armrests of his chair and peers at the space between Mother and Father, this close to understanding that a subtle shift in the room is becoming more heavily charged. Rachel withdraws her hands, and stands there swinging her hair back out of her face.

Dad looks at Jacob and asks, "Is that what you want? Do you want to leave Stonethrow, son?"

"No, Dad."

Beth grins in the past. She hissed in the present, and said, "Love."

Mom lifts her hands in a gesture of futility and glances at each of them as if expecting a prolonged explanation as to why no one else feels the world steadily growing out of control. "Jacob, I was only thinking you might like going to school with other kids your own age. You don't know it, really, but you're missing out on a lot. Junior high starts in the fall; I think you should go."

Rachel asks, "Is your friend pretty, Third?"

Jacob scans his sister's face, searching for mockery, but oddly enough, can't find any. Again, it's clear that she loves him, and he can't quite get over it. How much does she know, and does she feel that burning jealousy in her stomach, too, thinking about how others have come between them? He grits his teeth, his voice as flat as slate. "Yes, Rachel, very pretty."

"I'll bet she is, if she's a friend of yours."

Dad peers at him, moving around the bed and trying to see into the closet, but there're still Joseph's broad shoulders in the way. Mom stands there all agitated, doing a little nervous dance of anxiety, Jacob shifting over more and more. "What is she like, son?"

"She's my friend; she's nice."

His father takes another cautious step forward, and clears a catch in his throat. "Jacob? What is she wearing?"

"A dress."

"What color?"

There's an edge there in Dad now, and Jacob turns and looks over at him. "Why are you asking that?"

"Tell me. Is it yellow?"

"Isaac, what are you doing?" Mom asks, using that same tone to admonish Dad.

Jacob freezes. So Dad knows.

It's the time to talk of secrets—maybe they all should see her; the moment's come to turn out the pockets of their hearts and show each other just what's been going on inside. His head starts hurting again. Rachel and Joseph are too quiet; there's so much happening in the house for so much silence. *But the Raccoon bends her . . . Thrush slipping in the mud to reach up and glide lips against their bellies.* He hears a storm somewhere far away, a distant pummeling of thunder that rattles the houses on Beth's side of the board. The man he will be offers no advice. Jacob wants to wipe that puzzled look off of Mom's face. He's tired, with a tingling in his fingers, his temples, hearing those same croons of the muses; they never stop—not even when his brother and sister are hurtling through the forest.

"Yes, Dad," he responds weakly. "A yellow dress."

Elizabeth mimics being a fashion model

and makes exaggerated movements, holding her dress out in various poses, posturing for photographers, pouting for the camera. No, she's not Taddy's daughter.

"Have you been in my study, son?"

"No."

"Reading my stories?"

"I stopped reading your stories when you stopped showing them to me."

Dad at least has enough sentiment to wince at that, recognizing a fact when it's thrown in his face; he's been cutting his son off little by little for the last couple of years, but there are larger, more dangerous truths involved. "I want you to stand up and come to me, Jacob."

"Why?"

"Isaac, what's wrong?"

"Now, do as I ask now, please."

Beth shakes her head no.

Beth shook her head no, and held her hands out to him. The black half-moon rings beneath her eyes deepened to another frightful shade of darkness and sickness, death and beyond death. "I need you; I love you, my Lucifer." Jacob forced himself to stare into his own past, fighting back ten years of loss.

Rachel steps closer now, curls her fingers around the closet door and swings it open a little wider, another inch or two.

Elizabeth cringes. "They're going to hurt me."

"Jacob, stand up and come here!" his father shouts with the same intensity as when screaming for him to get out of the study.

Now is when the animal sounds are heard: Jacob grunting, Mom making a move as she croaks like a toad, Dad growling, Rachel giving a satisfied, prolonged groan, Joseph doing nothing if not seething and hissing. Everybody suddenly acting like abandoned creatures left to die in the street, or alone in the woods. Maybe, second by second, they're all growing aware of what is coming next, and next after that, and what will soon be rolling across the floor.

Maybe, before it happens again, he can stop it from happening the first time.

In the back of the closet, Jacob stood with Beth, as she moved closer and writhed against his back, her hands reaching forward to his belt buckle. She spun him away from the unfolding visions of his history, tore at his shirt, and bit into his chest. Her nails were like talons before his eyes, licking down the trail of blood. The ink washed against his skin like cold compresses. He said, "No, damn it." Her diseased face had become much worse in the last few minutes, until she was peeling.

"My love," she said.

"Son," Dad snarls in anguish, shoving past Mother, who simply stands with her mouth hanging open, her hands flailing. Rachel pulls the closet door open another inch, smiling broadly as she moans almost as if she were humming. Jacob knows her sounds: she's on the verge of orgasm. Dad takes another step; there is drama in every line of his face, each motion as he stalks closer. Joseph is wedged between the desk and the bed and Dad can't get through that way; he needs to shuffle past on the other side, but seems to be scared— it'll bring him behind Rachel and the closet door, and he'll be unable to face what he wishes to confront. He hops onto the bed, takes two bouncing steps, and leaps off past Mom.

He stares at Beth.

"Oh, my Jesus," he murmurs. "It's true; it's all true."

Rachel hauls back on the closet door, shoving it open all the way until the knob cracks against Joseph's armrests.

"She's beautiful," Rachel says breathlessly, shuddering, and Mom's eyes widen farther than they should, her eyebrows almost falling off her face as they will on her ghost ten years from now . . . and right now. His brother has on a proud yet sour face, as if thinking to himself how the kid has had his own little cream puff stored away all this time; no wonder he didn't need any of the muses.

Joseph looks down at Beth sitting by the Monopoly board and wants her for himself.

"What's true?" Jacob asks Dad, knowing that in the house everything is a lie, and will be for another decade.

Stunned, gaping from his son to Beth and back again, and never glimpsing the other Jacob far off in the darkness, he says, "That you were stealing from me."

"Dad . . ." Jacob nearly wails *Daddeeeeee* because he needs to, because it is the way he feels. "I never stole from you. I never go into your study." The seething starts: already ostracized from the rest of the world, locked away like a beast, he's lost whatever communion he once had even with his family. There are fragments of his shattered nose bones still in his brain, and he feels them scraping together.

He watches the faces of his family and can read their souls so clearly; amid all the emotions, he sees that they're all finding pleasure in this. Isn't there any torture, any of his agony that they can't find pleasure in? His father touches him on the shoulders and starts massaging there, moving up to the base of Jacob's neck to all the horror knotted in his migraine. Dad uses his strong hands to help unwind the snapping springs in Jacob's head, but it's not working.

Still not a part of the crowd, the only one remaining left out, Mom speaks up. "Isaac. Who is that girl? How did she get here? Somebody tell me what's going on! Rachel!"

Everyone ignores her. Joseph tugs at Rachel's arm so that he can pass by. His surprise and envy are so clearly presented in the curl of his lip; he wants to know how Jacob did it without his siblings, how was it that his need alone was great enough. Rachel's glare is equally readable; it's so clear she's finally admitting that Jacob never needed them in the first place, outside of spilling his blood.

His brother and sister both reach out to touch Elizabeth.

She shrieks and leaps up, cringing in the darkness, as if she might back into her wasting other self and the older Jacob. "You promised. . . ." she whispers, which strikes him harder. Her voice snaps him from the reveries brought on by Dad's tender hands working the migraine.

He stares into his father's face and can only ask, "Why are you killing me?"

Grabbing Jacob by the shirt collar, Dad gropes and tries holding his son without really touching him . . . like carrying a dead rat out into the trash. "Oh, God, no, never, Jacob."

"You've dried up. I know you have. I see the way you act. I hear the typewriter. You can't do it without me anymore."

His father nods, shame seeping into his face. "Only lately. The past couple of months." He shifts his bleary eyes to Beth. "Son, come away from there now . . . Please, oh, God, Jacob, please . . ."

Pouting and beautiful, Elizabeth says, "Go to hell."

Cupping her hands around her mouth, as if that might help her to be heard, Mom hollers, "Hey, would someone be so kind as to . . ."

Explain it all at this point? Dad holds his empty hands out to Jacob. "The girl is a character in a book I haven't been able to finish. Her name is Elizabeth O'Malley. She died of yellow fever in 1870 when she was ten years old."

"She's my friend."

"I know what you dream, Jacob," Dad says, and the room chills; even Rachel shivers. There's just something about the way he said it, as if he knows everything. Beth takes a step backward. "I've felt you tugging at my mind for weeks now. I didn't understand it at first, but now . . . it makes sense. These nightmares I've been having, of animals, of the woods talking. The words, the writing hasn't been mine, perhaps, but you've been inspiring me, regardless. That's what you're doing, son; you're reading images off my mind, taking them out of my imagination. She's not real."

Of course, what else could he expect? Dad wants her, too.

Jacob takes his time, working the hatred as he raises his arm and extends his index finger to point squarely into his father's face. "Get out of here, you. . . ." he whispers, and turns as Rachel grasps him, either hugging or wrestling, he can't be sure, but knows only that Beth is afraid and his sister's musk is overpowering, even here in his room. Her hair hangs partially in her eyes, and he reaches out to sweep it over her shoulder. Despite his brother's evil grimace and all their rising needs, Jacob struggles to get into the closet with Beth, but Rachel holds him tight, even now as Father falls upon him, too, the squeal of the tires loud as Joseph rolls forward, and Mother keeps shrieking, always out of the act except for now, as she closes the distance between them.

In his mind he screams one word, falling back into Rachel's arms, all of his nerve endings firing at once: *Fetch*.

A soul-piercing screech erupts from her, as she lifts her arms out to her sides and twirls, whirling as if dancing, her jaw hanging slackly as she wheels past Joseph's reaching arms and spins out through the bedroom door.

"Save me," Beth urges.

Jacob, with his fists full of Elizabeth's decaying skin—large, heavy flakes like sheets of paper, veins scrawled like words—let her flesh fall free from his hands as he stared out through the closet at his own memories. "It *was* my fault," he said. "I knew it; I *knew* it."

And then Jacob has his arms locked behind him, his elbows straight and hitched all the way up in the wrong way, nearly to the breaking point. He squeals like Joseph has squealed down in the mud. In the closet, Jacob grimaces, remembering the incredible pain. His brother has Jacob's arms gripped tightly in one of his massive hands, the other fist coming around to scrunch his jaw until they're able to look into each other's eyes.

"What are you doing to her? Bring Rachel back."

"I will."

It's a masterwork of understatement. *Bring her back,* as if he could ever let her go, as if she would ever let any of them go. How different it is under the blazing sun down by the edge of the pond, when the muses prance from the forest, and Rachel reclines against a log with her legs spread for one of them, whoever comes crawling through the silt to be with her.

Yes, they will pay for this travesty. Just look at how Joseph can't keep his eyes from Beth, his thick tongue hanging like a slug from his mouth; he can't help himself—this is what's been wrought in the maelstrom.

Mother, outside this awful circle, is still a part of it, and shows her love, screaming, "You're breaking his arms! Stop it, Joseph! Isaac! Isaac!" Dad stands wobbling, about to faint, unable to tear his gaze from Elizabeth, who has existed as perfectly as this in his thoughts, written up in his notes. Mom can't possibly loosen Joseph's hold, but takes off her shoe and smashes him across the bridge of his nose with the heel. Again and again, battering him across the neck and shoulders. He finally lets go, but not because of that—

his nose bleeds, framing his lips in crimson. He licks, and he licks.

Blood spatters down the armrests until it drips in a spear point over the spokes. Joseph's broken nose continues to gush as if a faucet has been turned on. What beautiful poetic justice, Jacob thinks, recalling the day when it all began in the pond, when he touched the fish.

He's going to do it again. *Christ.* Jacob fell to his knees, wishing he could climb forth from the ink and confront himself, watch the kid turn and walk to the window, the breeze ruffling his hair. Behind him, Beth hung upon his back like all the crosses he deserved to bear, the weight of his sins driving him down into the darkness. "I used to love you," he said, or perhaps it was she who spoke. Beth, the ghost child from fiction, still seated at the Monopoly board, turns and looks back at him, smiling.

The breeze billows the curtains, and Joseph rolls forward again, leaving tire tracks of blood. He seems almost ready to kill Jacob and Dad, wanting to covet Beth that badly, enraged that she doesn't have eyes for him.

"Succubus," Dad says. "I won't let you take my boy away."

It's so decisive, dramatic; you can almost

hear the thrum of Mozart in the background, orchestra swelling, the brass horns holding, and the oboes kicking in as Dad moves forward and grabs Jacob by the arm, pulling him and trying to stop the hideousness of all that's going on, to keep the evil from gorging on his family. He doesn't understand it's the family that is eating. For a minute he almost seems to have power, strength, and best of all, acumen, as though he finally understands what is occurring inside the maelstrom, and can counter and fight it.

"This is all my fault," his father says. "If only I could have figured it out sooner. If only I hadn't been so afraid."

He grips Jacob by the throat and hauls him forward, lifts his wife and tries to get her to move for the door. Fight-or-flight instinct takes over, so his father is running. Mom wobbles her feet, and says with genuine alarm, "What in the hell is happening?"

Dad points a finger at Joseph and shouts, "Out!" Joseph slams the closet door, but it bounces back open, and he starts rolling from the room.

Perfect timing, actually.

Flattened against the hallway wall and sobbing hysterically, Rachel turns and enters, swinging the ax.

The blow catches Joseph high in the left shoulder, and contrary to what Jacob remembered from the other side, his brother doesn't shriek. They all scream except for Joseph, who only gives a slight grunt, his eyes filling with an odd puzzlement, as if he can't quite believe so much has happened in so little time.

The blade sticks in his clavicle, and Rachel has to seesaw it back and forth a few times before she frees it from his body. Each groan he makes is met by one of her own, as if this is just another brand of their lovemaking. Blood sprays into both their faces, and she raises the ax above her head, getting a better grip on the handle. With his hands on the tires, Joseph tries to wheel himself out of her way, but there's a hesitation there, as though he's unconvinced she can be doing this to him, and a frown creases his brow despite the pain. His arrogance is overwhelming, as though he might will his major arteries shut. He wipes his bleeding nose with the back of his hand, as if that's more important. He sets his lips together, the sneer almost completely snapped back in place.

Rachel grimaces and drops her head back, perhaps aroused or resisting, her breasts outlined so wonderfully as she lifts the ax higher and higher, giving him all the time in the world to roll out of the way. It's defiance more than anything that keeps him there, as if he's daring her to do something she's already done.

She swings down, splitting his head in half.

In the closet, Beth laughs, and even rotting she laughed, and Jacob froze at the sound. He couldn't remember what he felt as a kid, and studied his own young countenance as Dad drags him from the room.

His brother is dead.

Rachel has become horrifyingly sane, despite the fact that she's shivering, flicking her tongue. She stares as if just waiting for something else to happen, somewhere else she can go. The blood of her lover trails off her eyelashes, and pitter-pats down her cheeks like tears.

Dad draws up short and stares, and puts out his hand to stop the slowly listing wheelchair from rolling backward into them. Mom finally realizes something is terribly wrong here; a shattered skull and leaking brainpan are enough to get her attention. She begins hyperventilating, sucking breath like the fish that began all this. She pleads. "Honey? God, Rachel, God, oh, God, honey?" She takes one fervently lurching step toward her daughter, as if she's about to do a Fred Astaire slide, arms wide open, before Dad has a chance to pull her back.

Rachel swings and chops their mother in the side of the neck, half burying the blade but not quite fully decapitating her.

Mom is still alive, maybe, her chest shrugging for air, her eyes rolling until only the whites show, falling backward nearly into Jacob's arms. He stretches out to grab her, screaming. Rachel tugs the ax and their mother surges forward, nothing but meat sticking to metal now, only a thin piece of gristle attaching her head to her body as she clumsily drops to her knees, inch by inch sagging, and violently slumps over. When her chin strikes the floor, her face spins like a party favor until at last the trail of viscera snaps, sending her head slowly rolling under the wheelchair.

His mother is dead.

You can tell that Dad is caught between holding Jacob up before him like a shield and shoving his son out of the way, perhaps hoping to protect him, perhaps hoping only to kill him. How can anyone watch this and remain rational, his father so stern and—maybe he's sane—simply inspecting Rachel as if studying some kind of newborn animal taking its first fumbling steps.

"It's not you, Rachel," Dad tells her, and she moans, a sound so deliciously erotic that Jacob moans, too, thinking that he can have her again; maybe things will be all right now, somehow. His father's voice is full of passion, just about the only time anybody has ever heard him like this outside his novels. "In my story Elizabeth is a ten-year-old ax murderer," he says.

From the closet, Beth shouts, "Bullshit!"

Wavering on her feet, Rachel whines like a dog for a moment, blinking wildly as the blood on her hands coagulates. Dad really hasn't done anything to stop her, realizing that he can't. Her hands make loud sounds like paper ripping as she shifts her grip on the sticky ax. She is more beautiful than Jacob can remember ever seeing her before, even at the pond: standing here like this with the sweat beading her forehead, fighting, and yet enacting what had to be done in the maelstrom.

His father shakes him firmly, but almost with a soothing touch. "Jacob, stop this. Let go. Let her go. Stop it."

So strange to hear it like that, because he never wanted anything to start; they'd forced his hand. His father shudders once, wavering as Rachel takes a step closer, something going on way in the back of her throat that might be stilted words begging forgiveness, or snarls, or more likely insults.

"Stop her. Don't let her do this."

As if it weren't already done, as if they could just mop the floor and put together the pieces and things could continue on from here without any trouble. "I want to, Dad. Help me."

"Do it, son."

Jacob's voice cracks as he cries, "Daddy," all the hope of his life tied up in his father, praying the man can make it right again.

Isaac Maelstrom knows he has no choice but to kill his son, though it's too late.

Jacob knows what Dad is thinking; he can see it in his own eyes as he stares at himself hiding there at the back of the closet, far removed from his bedroom now. He breaks his father's grip with a vicious movement, falls to the bloody carpet, and crawls under the bed.

Rachel spins with an animal grace and unbelievable speed, leaping forward like some wonderful martial artist, and swings, and swings. Their father backs away, still not looking very scared, as if this is only a dress rehearsal of a performance he knows so well

he doesn't even have to make an effort anymore. Rachel's hair flaps around her shoulders, strands sticking to the dried blood, as
she feints and Dad dodges, stepping carefully
around the corpses sprawled beneath them,
both of them looking like they might stop to
play Monopoly any second.

Rachel has gotten used to the weight of the
blade, the finely arcing momentum of the
rhythm of the ax, extending it farther and farther, with a frightening weave in the air, as if
the handle itself melted beneath her touch.
Isaac Maelstrom stifles a cry of fear as Rachel
wheels and swings, chopping him in the left
arm. His eyes widen, his mouth quivering as
he grimaces, wishing he could blame someone else besides his own stories for this. He
drops to the wall and Rachel sniffles, a little
girl with a cold wanting Daddy to take her in
his arms and cradle her to sleep.

He holds a hand over his wounded arm,
trying to keep the arterial spray from painting
the walls, and in a few seconds he is so dizzy
he flops forward onto his belly, dropping with
his cheek pressed to the carpet, inches away
from his wife's unfurled tongue. Dad gropes
for Jacob's hand, extending his blood-
sheathed arm under the bed, and through it
all Jacob reaches for his daddy.

Jacob nearly wails *Daddeeeeee* because he needs to, because it's the way he feels. For an instant there almost appears to be a reckoning of some sort. Neither of them smile, but there's something equally forgiving in their eyes, although it's clear the man would still kill him if he could, and perhaps that's how it should be.

Rachel brings the ax down across their father's neck.

Dad is dead.

Rachel hands him Joseph's head, that stern look of resignation still etched into the paling flesh.

She offers him their mother's head, tentatively, as if his sister wants to keep this one and place it somewhere special, upon a different altar. She hands him Dad's head, emptied of all the horrors and ghosts.

After she locks him in the closet, he hears her steps as she leaves the room and walks down the hall. Elizabeth laughs and buries her face in his chest, both of them fondling the faces of that which had once been his family.

Hours later, there is a shuffling of feet . . . a stench of fetid breath, body odor, and recently accomplished sex, all of them filling the room, moaning and weeping, imploring as they move purposefully among the deceased still swirling in the maelstrom . . . a soft knock at the door, as if not wanting to awaken those within, followed by the fumbling of the key . . . and a pink fist reaches in and hands him his sister's head . . . and then slowly, receding like the night, they leave the room and return to the forest to settle into the lovers' mud . . . and at long last he can finally find solace and sleep in the arms of Beth, and know the freedom, comfort, and eternal affection that is his own death.

# Chapter Twenty-seven

"Okay, enough of this bullshit."

Lisa figured there was no place to run or hide, nobody on her side now that she'd been abandoned and left to the house. It didn't even matter much that her neck and jaw made crackling noises, or that her heart hammered so hard it hurt her chest, or that her vision had taken on a bright and strange tinge, like she might pass out any second. Not a whole hell of a lot mattered anymore, except getting out of here.

She threw the door open, wondering where the metal would strike her first—in the belly to kill the child, or across her breasts to show power, or between the legs to make way for further rape. It skittered out there in the hall, footplates flapping up and down, zagging to get in front of her but not quite able to do it. The tire just brushed against her leg. It looked like a taxi, waiting for her to get in so that it could reel off for the airport.

Rachel and Joseph weren't warm anymore.

So much less solid now, they passed in front of her almost without even touching her. Their hands were white and wasted, as they moved around her silently for a moment, and then, straining, she thought she could hear them. *Return to us, Lisa.* She nearly burst out laughing. That's what they were going to say? Joseph's voice had a lilt, as if from Rachel's tongue. *You'll want it from us, Red. This is what's waiting for you.* The wheelchair seemed to be losing energy, too, a symbol of their union, with her pushing him everywhere and then getting a reward for her submission. It simply bumped and thumped, like a deranged person standing there and just clunking his own head back against the wall, frustrated with impotency.

"You're pleading," she said, astonished, and then suddenly the hate shook her until her bottom lip quivered. "With me? You're pleading with me!"

Sickened, she walked to the stairway as they followed, nearly transparent but with a sad, cooing sigh in her ear the whole time. The steps hadn't been here last time, the house warped and reshaped by their urgency. Now it remained solid, molded by her own desperation. Their ghosts tried for flesh, occasionally shifting in hue—she'd catch a glimpse of tooth and eye in there sometimes, the two of them hovering around her. Lisa forced herself not to listen to the humming tune they sang. She kept moving, taking two steps down at a time, but lost her footing on the worn-out carpeting and nearly slipped.

That wrenching caused more grinding in her neck and back, and she twisted sharply, sucking in air, and grabbed for the banister. She thought they might laugh at her for that, but they didn't. Joseph's hands seemed to reach out as if to help. Madness, but what difference did that make? She said, "Get away from me, you bastard."

Her forehead was bleeding again, and she

felt the hot fluid running into the corner of her eye. She swallowed her groans but didn't slow down, trying to keep count but losing it, still unsure which floor she'd been on.

But what to do now? She had to get to the car. To the road. To the bridge, and back to Bobby, or anywhere.

"Out?" she said, and let loose with that same heinous titter; now it seemed to be more of someone else than of her. They'd left her here to die, the happy couple, so busy with themselves in the bowels of the house, walking through walls, in the playground of corpses. "How is it out? That fucker just put a tree down; I know it."

The hot seat caromed off the railing behind her, convulsively banging back and forth into furniture behind her. She heard the wallpaper ripping and got a sordid satisfaction out of that, the house killing the house. One tire smashed loose and came spinning down past her in a leisurely roll, bouncing as it went by.

She hit the bottom step and swerved into the foyer, trying to get away, that familiar panic settling back in—she'd missed it for a while—and raised her arms in an attempt to defend herself.

The wheel came for her face, but she tripped over something small and dropped to all fours in time to keep the broken spokes from gouging her eyes. The rest of the chair tumbled and crashed into the front door, blocking her in.

"Nice try, kids."

*Stay.*

"Quit begging me like that!"

*Red-hearted bitch.*

"Hey. Hey, that's better, baby."

She looked down and saw that she'd tripped over the turtle.

It retracted its head into the shell, and she drew a finger down across its back. "Thanks, pal."

*Why are you here?*

She snickered. "Now, there's the question." She wondered which of them called to her, who wanted her more, and why this badly. Joseph's muscles rippled, the veins standing out on his forearms when she could make him out, wavering in the air. He made gestures of warm embraces, Rachel running her fingers across his chest, as if trying to hold him in place with her.

Lisa scrambled forward, grabbed the mangled seat by one of its armrests, and heaved and pulled, trying to get it the hell away from the front door. No good; she moved to the window, grabbed something, a hatrack or a coatrack, one of those stupid things you only found in a madhouse like this, and swung it against the window. The glass cracked but didn't shatter.

As she pulled back for another swing, the weakness suddenly swept back into her, all of it dropping on her at once like from out of a tree, each bruise and scrape and click of bone, the baby inside her maybe dying, maybe already dead—so strange to want to preserve it now, when yesterday she'd felt only alarm and dread.

She staggered and limped, unsure of where there was to go anymore, who to fight, who her friends were, or what to do. You were supposed to be able to call on somebody now, at times like these—God, or your guardian angel, your grandmother, or a righteous and defiant priest, somebody to come help you out. Rain splashed through the cracks, and she saw eyes in the dark.

"Help me," she said.

Fingers, or branches, scratched at the window, and shards of stained glass plinked back inside.

Agony skewered through her, vertically; a spear stabbed down deep through her neck, impaling each part of her inch by inch. She lay on the floor as the wraiths circled her, Jo-

seph and Rachel not even contemptible anymore, they looked so pathetic and wasted.

*Stay with us.*

In the haze of agony remained one small,
clear spot of terror where she could still think
rationally. It kept throwing her, the way they
were pleading. Why were they doing that all
of a sudden, no longer warm and bloody, with
that rage and lust in their faces? Now just
whispers in the wind, they traipsed around
the room like kittens, occasionally appearing
and then vanishing. Gritting her teeth, she
sucked wind hard, where it whistled through
the blood clots in her nose. "Look . . . you assholes . . . you ought to know that I'm not stay-
ing here, no matter what happens."

Slowly, with all the tugging of damaged
muscle in her back pulling her askew, Lisa
stood and managed to haul the wheelchair
slightly out of the way. She drew the front
door open just far enough so that she could
squeeze through, leaving trails of blood on
the jamb.

She didn't know where the keys to the car
were, but they wouldn't be in the ignition or
stuck under the sun visor; she didn't know
anybody outside of the movies who actually
did a stupid thing like that.

She just needed out of the house. She'd

make it to the road, at least that far; better to die any place else other than the house.

Lisa staggered toward the pond.

The deceased—as if remembering sunlit summer days of madness and joy—hissed, giggled, and followed.

Rain touched the child's skin.

Inside the foyer, the turtle showed its face.

Strange to think that even after all that had happened to him and his family, Jacob had never thought of death with any true sense of reality. In its execution, suicide did not seem to be an ending so much as a form of protection, an escape from persecution . . . a saving of the soul.

How scared could you be if your own god murdered himself on a plank?

"Hold me," Elizabeth cooed, and he didn't want to fight much anymore; she truly was so beautiful that he felt a flood of joy whenever he looked at her, despite the disease. He held her and heard a tightening sound, like flesh worming back into place. Now she no longer seemed ill, the dark circles gone from under her eyes, that drawn face having smoothed and filled out again.

The questions got to be staggering, but they

continued hammering. So what was the truth? Had he created her, the anima from his soul, and stuck her away in the back of his mind until he needed her again? That seemed reasonable, but so did the idea that she had actually been a creation of his father. The man had thrived on sticking his thoughts into others' heads. What mutant neurotransmitters had slithered inside his own father's skull? Elizabeth, a force of nature, a nymph from out of the soil of Stonethrow? Or the remainder of some dead child who'd wandered out of town and died here, strewn among the leaves but never at rest? There were demons you could make a pact with that would go and collect from strangers instead. It happened.

*Characterization,* Dad had said, *is the most important element of your art. Your people have got to be born but set free to change and grow; otherwise they'll be the same stuffed doll—from story to story they'll be the same.*

Beth—his girl, his lady, his best friend, this succubus made real and made hungry—and she looked at him with tears forming. She said it again, insisting, "Hold me."

"Of course," he said, hugging her.

"Tighter."

"Yes."

"I love you." She sighed.

"You just want me to die."

"Yes." Beth drew him out to arm's length, peering into his face as if looking for a vestige of something that had already fled. The bow was still a little crooked, and he reached up and righted it in her hair, the silky feel of it only a reminder of all that wasn't real in his world. A frenzied sea of typewriter-ribbon ink splashed against his legs. *Words fail.* She grinned, and the angles of her face deepened and sharpened, her teeth white and inhumanly perfect, so much like an animal's now, as her smile kept widening, her eyes glazing over with oddity and slaughter. Her giggle thickened until it was another voice that contained all the spiked edges of a cackle. "Yes. *Die. Die. Die.*"

From behind them, someone said, "Like hell."

Katie brought the wooden sword down and drove it through Beth's chest, where more ink burst from the empty space of her heart and into his face.

He threw back his head and howled from the pit of himself.

Beth curled at his feet, mouthing his name with the black pouring off her lips, and continued to stare at him, afloat on the ink rippling beneath them. Soon his pulse beat again squarely in his own wrists, and he saw that there was nothing left of her, not even the yellowing pages of his father's manuscript.

*Good-bye, my lady.*

# *Chapter Twenty-eight*

Katie pitched sideways as a hanger struck her hard in the cheek, and she felt the weight of the wall on one side, Jacob's chest muscles pressing against her breasts. The solid ground came pressing up against her feet, and the materialism of the moment was almost enough for her to faint from relief.

She checked her skin for ink stains and found none. Her legs quivered, that sense of displacement easing out of her slowly as his arm wrapped around her shoulders and walked her out into the bedroom.

Maybe he was crying, or choking, his voice so stuffed with meaning she couldn't tell what it meant. Katie looked up into his face and tumbled against him, grasping him, the two of them rocking for a moment.

He said, "Thank you."

It should have sounded inadequate, or uninspired, but it didn't. "Yes," she said, and waited.

"I . . ."

"Yes?"

"Give me a minute."

"We have plenty of time."

He scowled again. "No, I don't think that's ever true," he said, and kissed her lightly on the side of her face, tiny pecks working toward her lips, then with a little more passion, swinging his face down to hers. She collapsed against him for an instant, his arms making it better.

"Your mother gave me the piece of wood."

"And she told you what to do with it."

"Yes."

He waited for her to crumble, faint, or become hysterical—he was this close himself, and would have been raving if he were anyone but a Maelstrom. She was so incredibly strong; if only he had been as brave none of this ever would have happened. "It's going to be fine."

"We can leave now, can't we?"

"Soon."

She grimaced, the real etchings of terror creasing her face. Wouldn't it ever end? "That's not what I wanted to hear."

"It's not exactly what I wanted to say."

She called, "Lisa."

Lightning shredded the gloom. After the thunder had rolled past she cocked her head, straining, and thought she could hear someone singing, somewhere far off. It hit her again, just now, that feeling that everyone was out there in the forest together—Tim and the baby, Grandpa, the woman with the rosaries, Olivetti perhaps trying to soothe them—all of them at a party she hadn't been invited to.

He pressed her aside gently, as though he were at the party, too, and was going to go talk to somebody else on the other side of the room. She kept with him, though, like an annoying date, and took his hand. "What happened? Where's Lisa? Is she all right?"

"I'm not sure."

On the edge of hysteria, she sounded shrill

and bitter. "I thought it would be over; isn't it over?"

"No."

"They're still here? Your family?"

"Yes," he said, storming from the room as she followed urgently, trying her best not to cry anymore, and failing. He dragged her by the wrist. "They're here, Katie, inside me."

"Then—"

"They'll always be here, unless I manage to release them."

"And Lisa?" she said, wondering if he could free her, too, too scared to ask about herself.

He stopped and she saw the carved outline of the muscles in his back, the veins suddenly exposed on his forearms as he struggled not to scream in frustration. "She's beautiful. My brother and sister want to feed off her."

"Jesus Christ, where is she? What can you do? Stop them, can't you stop them? Just stop it!"

"Yes."

The implications of the scratches in his bedroom door didn't get past him, the tears in the carpet like the fingernails of a lover scratching down a sweaty back; the house had held them too long not to be affected. The familiar stench of their musk caught him high and hard, and he had to lean against the railing to catch his breath, feeling somewhat aroused and sick. Katie laced her fingers with his, and the two of them stepped around the guts of the wheelchair strewn all over the place, spokes and cushions and bolts scattered as if a four-car pileup had occurred. He couldn't believe the power of their desires, so formalized and slick, going after a girl even from the bottom of the deepest grave. Being coiled in flesh had given their lust form, but now where did their passions take them? They loved each other as man and woman, much farther into the kinks beyond brother and sister. Jacob had stopped hating and loving them a long time ago, and now the third had to come between them again.

"How are you going to do it?"

"I don't know yet," he told her.

"Where is she, can you see?"

"No, but I think she's in the forest."

"How do you know that?"

"Because," he said, "they're always in the forest."

Katie led, rushing for the door, and saw the wreckage of the banister, rips in the wallpaper, as if Lisa had tried to hold on and had been ripped away, the wheelchair lying in a heap blocking the door.

"I shouldn't have left," she sobbed. "Oh, God, I should've protected her."

Like the slit stirring from the pond he felt his rage convulsing within him, heard the cries of the muses in the woods now, preaching his name, the chanting and mutters. The nightmare lived in his bones. He'd murdered his family once but had failed to finish the job.

The migraine returned and he could feel the need to yelp for his mother; the wheelchair sighed and squealed, untangling as if yawning. Jacob grabbed its bent frame and mangled it further, both him and the metal hissing as Katie stared at the insane argument between himself and his brother's badge. He hefted and threw it out into the foyer. She took two steps, about to follow him out the door and into the angry night, when she tripped over the turtle.

It took one creeping step toward Jacob.

Katie sat up, dazed, and he lifted her to her feet. "Are you all right?"

"Don't leave me."

"You might be safer here."

He waited for her to damn him, to scream that it was all his fault, that she'd had enough troubles in life, she hadn't needed this, why had he done this to her, but she only said,

326

"Don't you leave me alone, Jacob."

"I won't." He took her hand and shoved through the screen door. It clattered shut behind them. "I'm going to burn this place to the ground."

"I'll bring the marshmallows."

Trees swung in the wind like gypsies performing rituals, fuming, pulling back as if wailing. The lawn stood high and ugly, littered with shingles and rotted branches, the dead flowers of his mother; twisted ironwork and shutters lay partially submerged in the swampish weeds. The face of the house loosened layer by layer. Wind hooked the woods and they reeled, everything moving wildly, with the clouds a slightly different shade of black tacked up against the spectacular dark, lightning cascading in wicked angles from earth to sky. Dwindling flames spewed through the brush, wind orchestrating the forest in a concert of moans. The slumping trunks of trees clashed, dominoing against one another, and unearthed roots sprang like hunters' traps.

As all circles close, Jacob felt certain the pond would be where the wheel would revolve back around. The three halves were bound to confront one another again there in the water; the world could grow no more mythical than that.

Katie kept up with him as they sprinted from the porch to the car. "My keys are upstairs."

"Mine, too. It doesn't matter."

"Do you see her?"

"No."

"Jesus." Her hair fell in drenched rings into her eyes. "Lisa!"

"We have to go to the pond."

"Why?" Maybe he was ready; maybe the dead were actually frightened of him. She didn't know exactly what she had done or what had been done to her. She hadn't frozen, though the memories were sticky things that clung but skittered, here and there, away from her when she tried to think of them. She mouthed, *Hold on, hold on,* meaning it for herself but more so for Lisa and him. They jogged down the muddy road together, and she grew nauseous down in the pit of her stomach, because despite everything, she had somehow never felt so in love before.

Lisa wondered what that other Lisa would think of this one here now: flopping in puddles, clambering in the slimy mat of leaves, her aching back throwing off all her movements and causing serious hitches so that she stumbled and wheeled, falling down. How far in front of the other Lisa was she—how far ahead of the flailing, pale siblings as she slid and rested on the bank of the pond?

She couldn't focus past the pain anymore, and lay gasping there, thinking that they might have beaten her, but she made them work for it. *Fuck them.* The baby, if it was still alive inside her, didn't need to know what kind of a mother she would have been, if she'd decided to have it at all. *Jesus, the blood.* Sharp rocks pressed into her side, and for a few seconds she drifted into a much warmer and more comfortable place, and then she was back, with her feet nearly in the water. Thunder brought the world rumbling around her again, that jagged grinding in her spine making her shudder and twitch. Her breath grew more shallow as she stared up, watching the lightning knife the sky.

Then came a face, grinning childishly.

For a minute she thought it was herself, staring down on her, about to cross her arms across her chest, one edge of her mouth drawn into a kind of ridiculous grin, the kind she gave when she felt like admonishing somebody a little. It was a trick she'd learned from her mother.

Right there above her, now stepping forward and lit by the flashes in the storm—a face framed by the branches of evergreen. She stirred and chewed her lip, ready for just about anything, seeing that it wasn't her own angry, petulant self but a man, bearded, wild and woolly, as if he'd been lost on the island, living in a cave someplace, and waiting for the lord of the flies to take him home.

From her angle she could make out that he had no shirt on, his chest a cross-thatching of welts and scars. Arched eyebrows and ugly ears, bottom lip hanging in a black vee. Her feet were cold, and she tried to drag them out of the water. Down in the dirt, with the wind bunching leaves against her side, she knew she looked like some hastily buried corpse.

He came around the line of brush, standing rigid as his hair whipped around him, naked and hairy, with nails grown out to claws.

"Hello," Raccoon said, bending to touch her on the shoulder, kind at first but soon much rougher. "Do you want me?"

A freezing spark flickered between his eyes as Jacob issued the command to scat—performing the old tricks. Raccoon moaned and gave him a *No, not again* look, taking his hand from Lisa's neck, where he had rubbed and tickled, straightening and suddenly scampering across the field screaming.

Could she be alive like that? Jacob went to his knees and pulled her from the water, so white with her face in the mire, hair matted on her forehead, and still so beautiful.

"Are you going to let us go home?" she asked, and Katie burst into tears.

"Yes," he said.

"When?"

"Now. Right now."

"Thank God."

Katie rushed from the shadows, sobbing, so much like Beth in her own way, another part of him through all of this. She slid and dropped beside Lisa, both of them staring into each other's faces before they hugged and the even deeper weeping started.

"Did you find what you were looking for?" Lisa asked.

"Who the fuck knows?" Katie said. She preoccupied herself with the notion that Lisa didn't look like she was dying, and that she was growing healthier every second. "How do you feel?"

"That's the dumbest thing you've ever said to me."

"Really?"

"I think."

331

"Answer me anyway."

"I feel like shit."

"Can you stand?" he asked.

"No."

"Rest there."

"What great advice."

"You'll be fine," he said, meaning it.

The muses watched in the woods.

His brother and sister were near.

"They want you," Lisa said.

"They want us all."

The delicious anger came back to him then, in one suddenly sweet moment, as he felt their wet mouths licking at the back of his brain. They called him. They were always calling him. The force of their presence weighed heaviest now, as they drew themselves from the force of his own being. In the base of his neck that familiar sensation began, the tightness in his forehead alerting him to the nightmare about to drag him down into it all over again. He dropped forward and sputtered, his pierced brain squirming, his fingers and crotch on fire.

Rachel's long black hair curled in that way she had worn it on holidays. So everyone knew they were at a point they would never come back to again. Where were Mom and

Dad? Joseph stood glaring, his massive arms and legs corded and solid.

*Come back to us, Third,* Rachel told him, her voice quickly thickening into reality. He'd never heard her beg before. "You can be with us."

"I know what happened."

He could imagine his father typing this scene, each of them playing it out from the world, hell, and purgatory.

Joseph couldn't keep his eyes off Lisa. "Come on," he said. "It will be everything you always wanted it to be."

"You don't sound too sure of that."

Which of us is really Lucifer? Jacob wondered. Rachel wove against their brother, her palms roaming Joseph's back. Jacob could only imagine what it might be like to have someone love you as much as that. He felt a pang of admiration and jealousy. Whispers from the woods called their names, everyone having polished their lust for all these years, wanting to unleash it again. Joseph grinned, knowing exactly what was going on in Jacob's head, and soon Rachel tittered, a heinous groan that made her sound more dead than a final last gasp ever could have.

"Third . . ."

"It's over," he said.

She shook her head. "No, because you don't want it to be."

Mud sucked at Joseph's feet, angry, slurping sounds snapping as he took a few steps forward. His gaze shifted from Katie to Lisa and back again. "I'll bet she tells you that she loves you," he said, trying to throw in as much sarcasm as possible. He managed only to sound off with a puerile *nyeah-nyeah* whine. "But how good is that; how badly do you need that, after what you've had?"

"I love you," Katie murmured behind him. "I do."

Jacob nodded at nothing, the sky emphasizing exactly what he was feeling: electrical and aware. His forehead tightened again and he doubled over, the migraine digging in like the twisting hooks of his own bones. Lisa's breathing gave him a rhythm to follow; Katie's sobbing kept pace with his pulse.

"Make love to me," his sister begged.

"Jesus Christ," he said. "Stop it."

There are deaths too long to be only deaths. You add together those things that need to be put together: like the panic and aberrant fluids slithering forward to the temporal lobe, eldritch moments of flesh and blood meeting in the heart of wrath. The black depths of the pond called to him. Jacob understood his position in the scale of nature in this instant. Rachel was now moving forward as she did before on the day they began to die, to reach out and put her hand on his neck, Joseph a maniacal vindicator, the three of them together as it should have been, as he turned back to the water.

All of the muses cry out from longing together, and it's an amazing sound. A blaze and a burning, as Jacob's fists clench and unclench, feeling himself fading once more. Dad wouldn't have written a happy ending. They milled about and circled him, like a naked pack of victims, singing that same song. He said, "Where's Ophelia?"

One of them pointed at his feet, and he spun and saw her lying there nearly hidden in the tall grass. Her yellow saucer eyes were on him, blinking in that loving way she had about her, sensuous and bright, their child in her arms.

"What did you expect?" his brother said.

The baby was dead.

"That doesn't mean anything to you," Rachel reminded him.

"Yes," he said, "oh, Christ, it does."

Ophelia held the child up to him, making an offering. She whimpered, "My liege, my liege," because it was all she could say. "My liege, my . . ." They held the baby between them, and he touched the spot where its forehead should have been, feeling the coolness there, the safety in the dead baby. His muses watched in silence. With the dwindling rain sweeping past them, Jacob didn't know who to turn to next. Grinning and as handsome as ever, Joseph seemed to have answers he didn't want to give.

Faces pressed close, noses sniffing his underarms, breasts bouncing against his Adam's apple. He felt their paws slapping him hard between the shoulders, like someone might hand him a cigar, waiting to look at baby pictures. They scrutinized him with animal gaping, the maelstrom continuing. In her arms, wedged against his chest, remained their heir—a sack of indecipherable child.

The only two words that might still hold any meaning for them—love and failure—collided here where they had first learned what passion truly meant. He looked back to see Katie and Lisa in the shadows, slowly becoming more and more separate from himself. Memories of his living siblings beat on the present, finding themselves corpses. This remained where they had discovered how inescapable the lovers' knot could become. The siren dream of Ophelia had given them the gift of poetry, and his baby had suffered for that need and lust. "We didn't fail, Ophelia."

She ran a finger over his lips and smoothed his eyebrows. "Do you love me?"

"Of course."

The darkness swirled, as Katie stiffened.

Ophelia smiled. "That's all I've ever wanted, Jacob."

She led him to an area already cleared, and they buried the baby together. Some of the muses helped in the digging, while others slept, and still others watched for the sunrise. The ignition of his nightmares came into focus, and he did for the muses what he wished God would do for mankind—he took back the fruit of knowledge.

Dwindling, noisy forms hopped and flew and ran around in circles, the brush alive with beasts that had been human, but pure. They keened and whistled, aware of him but unconcerned, neither thankful nor forgiving, but accepting both the gift and the curse of what he'd granted and taken back. Joseph and Rachel both gaped and took steps this way and that, as if they might gain in the return of innocence to the wild.

Shining scales reflected the slow crawl of dawn, and a swimming stare without eyelids that would never blink again looked at him for a moment, and was gone.

*Conclusions.* Dad had said. *Always finish with a fierce culmination, bloody or subtle, so long as there is a finality of purpose, but a resonance of action. Nothing leading to sequels. End is end.*

"You'll never know how sorry I am," he told his brother and sister.

Terrified perhaps of being touched, Rachel moved farther and farther away. "Be with us," she said.

"You've never been here."

"We know what you need," Joseph said, trying to keep control of his dread. "Someday you'll end up seeing us again. Listen to me, Third, you little prick, someday you'll see us again. We'll find you. We will! We'll find you!" He held their sister, and she at least was able to give a wry grin.

Without the flaming swords of angels or a chorus of demonic shrieks, without the sun rising too soon or any kind of miracle or rainbow to mark their passing from him, Joseph and Rachel fell away to a blazing afterimage, still smirking.

His brother and sister were dead.

He said, "I hope so."

\* \* \*

There are seconds too long but not long enough.

Katie moved to his side and then drifted away again, the wind rising a bit as the rain ended and the sunlight seemed to tumble from out of nowhere. It happened like this because it had to be like this. He tasted the scent of her gardens, as his mother came to walk among them again. Drawn from the dirt, he should have suspected she'd be dressed in her mud-covered Farmer Brown overalls, the aroma of the orchards clinging to her and bringing back startling yet happy memories. Was there a chance she looked happier than she did before, the edges of her mouth angled more toward a smile? She came to him and put her hands on his shoulders.

"Thank you," he said.

"Did you find us? Have you lost us?"

"Yes, but you've given me something more."

Mom did smile then, radiantly, as he always knew his mother could smile, with something so beatific in it, full of affirmation of the firmest kind. "Good, I'm glad." She kissed his cheek, and his mother's caring touch brought him to her with his arms open, his lungs aching as he began to weep. "We've

339

loved you; we've always loved you. It's never been your fault." He could smell the dirt of her.

"Do you forgive me?" he asked.

But she was already gone.

He had to face his father.

Silently, Dad sprang from the quickly receding shadows as if breaking free from his own notebooks. He was tall and lean, and his eyes remained remote and unreadable, guarded by all the pages of their entwined lives. Darkness ceased thrashing as the dawn broke harder, the man's feet enfolded by typewriter ribbons. There were a few tentative clacks of the keys, but then nothing, all the writing finished.

He stood before his father. How many times, in his average despair, had he begged for this reckoning? How often had he dreamed and demanded that his dad come back to him like this, blaming *him* for each of the terrors, this man who had once told him to get out of here? On those nights, after rereading the old manuscripts and balancing those plots side by side with his own, Jacob had flipped photographs like baseball cards, hoping to hear his dad again. So this was how the story of the ax-murdering ten-year-old

Elizabeth ended outside of the page. The meaning of it held true. Dad had said it so simply before, dedicating the purity, right at the beginning: *because.*

With the word came absolution. No pipe-organ death march, seething corpses in the ground. No crimes or punishments or further curses? He didn't know.

Isaac Maelstrom came forward and said, "It's not your fault."

"Yes, it is."

"No more than mine."

His father held out his hand then, a reserved man seeking to end this like a reserved man, nothing else passed down, no further legacy to invoke. Jacob couldn't imagine either of them letting it finish without an admission of love or hate, anger or guilt—with no catharsis. Shaking hands like strangers? Bile rose in his throat. He fumbled for something more to say, and stuttered. He stared into Dad's eyes and glimpsed speckles of remorse, and maybe pride. He had no choice but to give up the fury and accept everything that was left. He hid his face against his father's chest for an instant, like the boy he'd never actually been, his dad the demon slayer having given him the courage to confront the boy who'd been murdered in the pond. Jacob mouthed, "Don't go, don't go, don't go." So much more needed to be said, the sunlight bearing down on him until he was only holding on to Katie, Lisa standing and muttering, all the other devils he had known having found some peace, he hoped.

End might just be beginning.

Something crept over his foot.

He looked down and saw the turtle. It had heard, somehow, the music of the muses, and learned of the laughter, joy, and rapture of what it was to be human. He stared into its head and heard its complaints, begging to be touched.

Lisa's face showed exactly what she thought, and what would happen: how she'd never see Wakely again, or Katie for that matter, but simply leave in the night, keeping ahead of any other Lisa.

"Are you ready to leave here without them now?" Katie asked.

He almost said no.

# HEXES

## TOM PICCIRILLI

Matthew Galen has come back to his childhood home because his best friend is in the hospital for the criminally insane—for crimes too unspeakable to believe. But Matthew knows the ultimate evil doesn't reside in his friend's twisted soul. Matthew knows it comes from a far darker place.

___4483-8                                    $6.99 US/$8.99 CAN

# BENTLEY LITTLE
# DOUGLAS CLEGG
# CHRISTOPHER GOLDEN
# TOM PICCIRILLI

# FOUR DARK NIGHTS

The most horrifying things take place at night, when the moon rises and darkness descends, when fear takes control and terror grips the heart. The four original novellas in this collection each take place during one chilling night, a night of shadows, a night of mystery—a night of horror. Each is a bloodcurdling vision of what waits in the darkness, told by one of horror's modern masters. But as the sun sets and night falls, prepare yourself. Dawn will be a long time coming, and you may not live to see it!

-------------------------------------------------

# A LOWER DEEP
# TOM PICCIRILLI

A man known only as the Necromancer and his demonic familiar named "Self" wander the spectral highways of the countryside, incurring the wrath of both heaven and hell—and facing the curses of the damned. Jebediah DeLancre, the leader of the Necromancer's old coven, has now created a new coven, an evil band determined to use the black arts for their own hideous ends. The Necromancer is forced to return to his home, a place haunted by memories where years earlier his original coven was destroyed, and where Danielle, the only love of his life, met an awful death. The Necromancer and Self must battle not only his former master, but the members of the new coven and the jealous ghosts of his old one . . . all the while taunted by the possibility that Danielle may return from the dead.

# BRIAN KEENE
# RISING
### THE

Nothing stays dead for long. The dead return to life, intelligent, determined . . . and very hungry. Escape seems impossible for Jim Thurmond, one of the few left alive in this nightmare world. But Jim's young son is also alive and in grave danger hundreds of miles away. Despite astronomical odds, Jim vows to find him—or die trying.

**Dorchester Publishing Co., Inc.**
**P.O. Box 6640**
**Wayne, PA 19087-8640**
_____5201-6
$6.99 US/$8.99 CAN

Please add $2.50 for shipping and handling for the first book and $.75 for each additional book. NY and PA residents, add appropriate sales tax. No cash, stamps, or CODs. Canadian orders require $2.00 for shipping and handling and must be paid in U.S. dollars. Prices and availability subject to change. **Payment must accompany all orders.**

Name: _____

Address: _____

City: _____ State:_____ Zip: _____

E-mail: _____

I have enclosed $_____ in payment for the checked book(s).

_For more information on these books, check out our website at www.dorchesterpub.com._
_____ _Please send me a free catalog._

# YOU COME WHEN I CALL YOU

## DOUGLAS CLEGG

An epic tale of horror, spanning twenty years in the lives of four friends—witnesses to unearthly terror. The high desert town of Palmetto, California, has turned toxic after twenty years of nightmares. In Los Angeles, a woman is tormented by visions from a chilling past, and a man steps into a house of torture. On the steps of a church, a young woman has been sacrificed in a ritual of darkness. In New York, a cab driver dreams of demons while awake. And a man who calls himself the Desolation Angel has returned to draw his old friends back to their hometown—a town where, two decades earlier, three boys committed the most brutal of rituals, an act of such intense savagery that it has ripped apart their minds. And where, in a cavern in a place called No Man's Land, something has been waiting a long time for those who stole something more precious than life itself.

___4695-4                                    $5.99 US/$6.99 CAN

**Dorchester Publishing Co., Inc.**
**P.O. Box 6640**
**Wayne, PA  19087-8640**

Please add $1.75 for shipping and handling for the first book and $.50 for each book thereafter. NY, NYC, and PA residents, please add appropriate sales tax. No cash, stamps, or C.O.D.s. All orders shipped within 6 weeks via postal service book rate. Canadian orders require $2.00 extra postage and must be paid in U.S. dollars through a U.S. banking facility.

Name_____
Address_____
City_____ State _____ Zip _____
I have enclosed $ _____ in payment for the checked book(s).
Payment <u>must</u> accompany all orders. ❏ Please send a free catalog.

# INFERNAL ANGEL
# EDWARD LEE

Hell is an endless metropolis bristling with black skyscrapers, raging in eternal horror. Screams rip down streets and through alleys. The people trudge down sidewalks on their way to work or to stores, just like in other cities. There is only one difference. In this city the people are all dead.

But two living humans discover the greatest of all occult secrets. They have the ability to enter this city of the damned, with powers beyond those of even a fallen angel. One plans to foil an unspeakably diabolical plot. The other plans to set it in motion—and bring all the evils of Hell to the land of the living.

----------------------------------------------------

# MONSTROSITY
# EDWARD LEE

Blue skies, palm trees, and flawless white-sand beaches. Clare Prentiss thinks her new home is paradise, and her brand new job as security chief at the clinic almost seems too good to be true. It is. But the truth is worse than she could ever imagine.

Lurid dreams, erotic obsessions, and twisted fantasies aren't the only things that abruptly invade Clare's life. Is someone really peeping into her windows at night? Yes. Could those grotesque things in the woods possibly be real? Yes. Is Clare being stalked? Yes. But not by anything human. By a monstrosity.

-------------------------------------------------